Table of Contents

TWO OF A KIND -
The Beginning

GAIL MEATH

<u>**Jax Diamond Mysteries Series:**</u>
Songbird, Book 1
Framed, Book 2
Deuce, Book 3
Two of a Kind, Book 4, novella
Blackjack, Book 5
Killjoy, Book 6
The Diamonds, Book 7
Wildcard, Book 8 (April 2025)
<u>**Stone & Steele Mysteries Series:**</u>
A Perilous Premiere, Book One
A Bloody Banquet, Book Two (October 2025)

Bonnie DeMoss, Editor

Thank you to the Readers

I want to thank everyone for your time and interest in the Jax Diamond Mysteries series. I truly appreciate your support. I have had such fun writing this series. Yet, after I finished the third book, I was curious how Jax and Ace had met. I hope you enjoy reading about the beginning of their beautiful friendship...

Happy Holidays!

1

Wednesday, December 14

Officer Jax Diamond drove the patrol car down Essex Street, heading for the Lower East Side. It was after one-thirty in the afternoon, and he and his partner, Officer Tim Murphy, were still on duty in Manhattan. They had worked through lunch chasing a purse-snatcher, so they decided to sneak away to grab a couple of pastrami sandwiches at Ratner's Delicatessen.

"Let's make this quick, Jax," Tim told him. "If Captain Ryan gets wind that we left our beat, he'll put us on desk duty again."

"Would you relax? If he finds out, we'll just say we were tracking down another petty thief. That seems to be all we're good for these days."

"And whose fault is that? You're on pretty thin ice with the captain after spouting off at him at the meeting last week."

"Aw, c'mon, Murph, you know as well as I do that either Orin Marino or Digger Caputo hired that goon to clip the owner of the Blue Lagoon. My bet is on Marino since he owns the Pelican Club and had the most to gain by shutting the Blue Lagoon down. Digger Caputo is just a two-bit jewel thief, but they

4

both keep getting away with all sorts of crimes. They pay their lawyers a bundle of money, and their lawyers turn around and pass a good chunk of the dough off to dirty politicians in the city. Marino walked away scot-free from the Wall Street bombing last year, didn't he?"

"Yeah, but we didn't have any solid evidence against Orin Marino, Jax. Maybe you and I saw him at the scene of the bombing, but there were crowds of people there that day. You have a personal grudge against Marino, and the captain knows it. Everyone knows it."

"Well, all I know is that he's guilty as sin, and so is Caputo, and we should be tracking them, not wasting our time on stupid petty criminals."

"If you played by the captain's rules for once, maybe he'd start listening to you."

They both fell silent until Jax parked at the curb near the corner of Essex and Delancey. Tim told him that he'd be right back, but Jax knew differently. Jacob Harmatz, the owner of Ratner's, was a terrific guy but a real talker, and he'd keep Tim there for a good twenty to thirty minutes, rattling on about his wife and kids, and who knows what else.

While Jax waited in the car, he stuck his left arm out the car window and began tapping his fingers against the outside of the door in beat with some crazy jazz tune stuck in his head. He'd gone to Duke's Club last night and had a great time. The band had come up with several new songs, keeping everyone on the dance floor long into the night. He didn't get home until three o'clock in the morning, but he never slept anyway, and going to Duke's was a heck of a lot better than sitting home alone in his apartment.

Some yipping little dog in the neighborhood broke his thoughts, so he started whistling the tune and glancing around. The frigid temperatures felt warmer with the brilliant sunshine overhead, and everyone seemed to be enjoying the afternoon with the Christmas holidays next week. The store owners across the street were busy with customers, a group of kids played catch in the alley, and plenty of other folks leisurely strolled along the sidewalk in no hurry to get wherever they were going.

But that incessant yapping started grating on Jax's nerves. Scowling, he searched the area for the source. A lazy old basset hound slept soundly in front of the grocery store, and a big yellow retriever sat quietly in the alley, watching the kids play. Impatiently, Jax poked his head out the window for a clearer view.

As soon as a group of people on the corner crossed the road, Jax spotted the annoying little dickens making all the noise, and he burst out laughing. A black and tan puppy no bigger than a football stood by the front door to the Chase National Bank across the street. As he barked relentlessly, his stubby little front paws lifted off the ground like a Mexican jumping bean.

Jax relaxed in his seat, smirking. He figured the puppy's companion must have gone inside the bank, and the little rascal wouldn't settle down until they were reunited again.

A gentleman dressed in his finest duds, top hat, and cane walked across the street and approached the bank. The puppy followed the man's heels to the front door, obviously with the thought of slipping inside. When the man tried opening the door, it appeared to be locked or jammed. The dandy looked at his pocket watch, then he pulled the door handle again. When it still wouldn't open, he shrugged his shoulders and went his merry way down the road.

The puppy resumed barking.

Jax sat there for a minute, wondering about it. Finally, he got out of the patrol car and glanced towards Ratner's, but he knew Tim would be gone a while longer. He tossed his police cap and wool overcoat into the backseat of the car to better blend with the pedestrians. He headed across the street, keeping his eyes on both the bank and the puppy as he went.

After he reached the corner, he continued down Essex Street, deliberately avoiding the front door. He stopped beside the first arched window on the side of the stone building. With his impressive height, he could easily peek inside the window. At first, he didn't see anyone, not one teller or customer, which was puzzling in itself. Yet, he noticed the shadow of someone moving around farther back in the bank. He hurried over to the next window and discreetly looked inside.

A bank teller stood behind the counter with a man who Jax assumed was a fellow teller or the bank manager. He continued scanning the room, and a cold chill suddenly shot through him.

In the far corner, six people huddled together on the floor, and another man stood over them holding a gun.

Swiftly, Jax assessed the situation, trying to see if any of the hostages were hurt. That's when he noticed a dark-haired woman seated a few feet away from the others, crying and holding a young boy in her lap. Within seconds, she spotted him peering through the window, and the pleading expression on her face broke his heart.

Jax raced around the corner to the patrol call box in front of the grocery store. When the dispatcher told him to wait so he could call the Seventh Precinct and use the proper channels to report the crime, Jax furiously shouted at him to put him through to Captain Ryan of the Thirteenth Precinct. Thankfully, he intimidated the man enough that his call went straight through to the captain.

As Jax quickly explained the situation to his superior, he noticed the little puppy was sitting at his feet, quietly staring up at him as though waiting to see what he intended to do next. Tim stood behind him now, listening to his conversation. "I'm going to find a way in there, Captain!" Jax yelled. "There are nine hostages, and one of them is a young boy!" Captain Ryan started ranting and raving, ordering him to stay out of it and wait for reinforcements.

Jax slammed the phone down. "I'm not waiting!"

"Jesus, Jax, don't do anything stupid," Tim argued. "You heard the captain. I heard him, too. He said he'd fire you on the spot if you disregarded procedures one more time."

Jax stormed back across the street with both Tim and the puppy hot on his trail.

"You said yourself that the front door was locked," Tim went on. "There's no other way to get inside, not without alerting the robbers. That, alone, could push them right over the edge and..."

"There's a little boy in there, Murph! He looks about five years old. What if it was Lizzie? Wouldn't you want someone to do everything they could to save your daughter?"

"I wouldn't want someone risking *her* life trying!"

Jax ignored him and went over to the second window, but the pint-sized puppy scampered ahead of them and stood by the basement window well, wagging his tail excitedly. Jax hurried over and fell to his knees beside him. Five metal bars protected the basement window from outside entry, but he knew he could easily pry them away and break the window using Tim's overcoat as a buffer. That way, the crooks wouldn't hear anything. He quickly snatched his pocketknife and started digging around the top edges of the bars.

"Don't do this, Jax," Tim pleaded. "Your job is hanging by a thread as it is, and with the police commissioner, too. All they need is one excuse to pull your badge, and I don't want to lose you as a partner."

"Give me your overcoat, Murph," Jax told him.

"No!" Tim grabbed his arm. "C'mon, Jax, look at all the good we've done for the city. Don't throw it all away because of one stupid mistake."

Jax yanked his arm back and raked his hand through his hair. "We've got to do something…"

"But not this. Our precinct is only a couple of miles away. We need to wait for reinforcements so they can handle it the right way."

While Tim frantically kept trying to talk him out of it, Jax didn't know what to do. He loved his job, and he knew he was damn good at it. Sure, he'd crossed the line plenty of times before, but more often than not, his actions and hunches had been met with success. Yet, if he did anything stupid right now, just one wrong move, he would not only lose his job, but he'd be risking the lives of the hostages, including the young boy.

Just then, four patrol cars pulled up Essex Street behind them and parked a short distance down the road. Eight officers got out and headed towards them with Captain Ryan in the lead.

Jax rushed over. "Captain, let me go in by myself," he implored, trying to keep his tone in check. "I can slip through the basement window without being heard and convince them to put their weapons down and let the hostages go. You know it's safer for everyone if you send one man inside to negotiate with them instead of bursting in with an army."

"Stand down, Officer Diamond," the captain ordered.

Jax's face flushed as his temper flared. "Damn it, Captain, I can do this! It's the best chance those people have of getting through this without any injuries."

"I said, stand down!" the captain shouted, and they all marched to the back door of the bank.

When one of them lifted a crowbar to pry the door open, Jax groaned and squeezed his eyes shut, knowing this wasn't going to end well for the hostages. Even the puppy sitting at his feet started whimpering.

Tim stood beside Jax, and they both remained stiff and silent, watching from the sidelines to see how this played out. Within mere seconds after the officers entered the building, they heard several gunshots inside.

Jax bolted forward, heading for the second window and holding his breath until he saw two men lying on the floor, dead. A third man wearing a handkerchief that partially covered his face was in handcuffs and wincing with pain from a gunshot wound to his shoulder. As the officers helped the hostages off the floor, Jax caught sight of the woman and the little boy. She shook her head, refused the officer's help, and remained sitting there, cradling her son.

Jax rushed to the front door and impatiently waited for the officer to unlock it. Once done, he slipped into the building, flashed his badge, and hurried past the scared yet healthy hostages being escorted out of the bank. Captain Ryan had the wounded crook in custody. Only one of the dead men on the floor wore some sort of face-covering. The other one was in a security uniform.

Then Jax saw her...the woman with the little boy. She had finally agreed to leave the bank with one of the officers, but she was crying hysterically while carrying her bloody and lifeless son in her arms.

Jax fell back against the wall and held his head down, unable to face her as she passed by him. When he finally lifted his head, his damp blue eyes crossed paths with Captain Ryan's dark, remorseful gaze for a split second before the captain looked away and took the wounded prisoner out the front door.

Jax glanced over at the two dead bodies on the floor again. "Who are they?" he asked Officer Duncan.

"One of them is the bank security guard," he replied. "According to Captain Ryan, the other one is wanted for robbing two other banks in the city. His partner will do plenty of time for this."

Jax wandered outside. A crowd had gathered, but Tim was waiting for him. He handed Jax his overcoat, and they both stood on the corner watching the first ambulance slowly drive away with the mother and child inside.

As soon as it was out of sight, without a word, Jax crossed the street and headed down the sidewalk, away from the scene. He continued walking for five blocks until he caught the trolley for Brooklyn.

After he boarded, he sat down in an empty seat, and as the trolley pulled away, he saw the puppy sitting on the sidewalk, watching him leave.

2

"Fold"

Thursday, December 15

By dawn the next morning, Jax was still standing in front of the window in his living room, staring out into the darkness at nothing at all except the gutting memories of a mother's tears. Storm clouds had rolled in a few hours ago, and sheets of rain and sleet pelted the glass, magnifying the wretched image already embedded in his mind forever.

After he'd returned to his apartment yesterday afternoon, he locked the door and ignored the telephone, which rang off the hook. He refused to answer the door even when Tim pounded his fist against it, begging him to let him in.

Jax felt bad about avoiding his partner and best friend. None of this was his fault. Tim not only loved his job, but he relied on it to support his family. That meant following police procedures exactly, even when he disagreed with them.

And despite their many differences, he didn't entirely fault Captain Ryan either since he, too, undoubtedly had followed orders from his superior, the police commissioner.

Jax shouldered the bulk of the blame. He was furious with himself for being more concerned about the consequences of his actions rather than following his own instincts and doing what he felt was right. In his heart, he knew his plan would have saved the little boy's life.

He looked down at the small blue-eyed wooden figurine in his hand. It was a Christmas nutcracker dressed as a soldier in a navy and white uniform, with gold epaulets on each shoulder and a sheathed sword hanging from his belt. During one of Jax's brief escapes from the orphanage when he was twelve years old, a woman stopped him on the city streets and gave the nutcracker to him. He'd never seen her before or since, yet her words had never left him.

He set the nutcracker back on the table beside the window and went into the kitchen to heat a kettle of water. After he poured himself a cup of coffee, he stood by the window again until it was time for him to report for duty. Dressed in civilian clothes rather than his uniform, he took the subway from Brooklyn to the Thirteenth Precinct, located in the southwest portion of Midtown Manhattan. Once he reached his destination, he walked with a determined stride down the sidewalk. The rain and sleet had let up, although dark clouds still hovered overhead.

Jax quickened his pace when he reached the building, anxious to get this over with as quickly as possible. After he climbed the steps to the main office on the second floor, he took a deep breath and headed down the aisle. He passed by his desk and kept looking straight ahead. He couldn't be sure if it was his imagination or not, but it seemed the entire room of officers, a good fifteen or twenty of them, all fell silent as he walked towards Lieutenant Simmons' office.

Jax stopped and stared at the door as though it were the gates to hell. Once opened, he greeted the receptionist, a thin, almost stick-like elderly woman with gray hair pulled back so tight into a bun, it skewed her face. He tipped his hat to her. "Good morning, Alma. You're looking lovely today."

She smiled. "Hello, Jax. You're not in uniform. Did you finally take a day off?"

"Something like that. Is Lieutenant Simmons in his office? I need to speak with him for a minute."

"I'll see if he's available." She lifted the telephone receiver and pressed the intercom button. "Officer Diamond is here to see you, Lieutenant. Yes, sir." She looked up at Jax. "You can go right in."

Jax winked at Alma, entered the room, and found the lieutenant sitting behind his desk. "Thank you for seeing me, sir. This won't take long." He pulled out his police badge and handcuffs and set them down. "I appreciate having the honor of serving on the police force."

Lieutenant Simmons stood up, frowning. "You're quitting?"

"We both know it's best for all concerned." He laid a Smith and Wesson revolver down beside the other items. "I never used the department's gun since I prefer my own Colt pocket pistol."

"Hold on, Jax. I read the captain's report this morning. It was a tough call, and he's sick about it, too, but the surviving hostages have you to thank for being the first officer on the scene and alerting the precinct. It's all right there in his report. Why don't you take a few days to think about it? You haven't used any of your vacation time, and I'd hate for you to make a hasty decision regarding something so important. Take as much time off as you need. I'll put the approval through."

"That won't change anything, sir. I've made up my mind."

Lieutenant Simmons let out a heavy sigh as he came around his desk and stood before him. "Jax, you're one of the best officers I've seen in a long time. I know yesterday was hard, but you did everything you could."

Jax's jaw tightened, and he squeezed his fists. "Did I? Just before I called the precinct, the mother of the little boy inside the bank saw me through the window. You should have seen her face, Lieutenant, the look in her eyes. I'll never forget it for as long as I live. She was begging me to save her and her son. Instead, he died because I was too worried about losing my job. I doubt *that* was in the captain's report. So, no, I didn't do all that I could." Jax reached over to shake his hand. "Thank you, Lieutenant. I've enjoyed working for you."

Dolefully, the lieutenant stood there. "I hate to see you go. Officer Murphy can't be too happy about your decision, either. You've been partners for nearly three years."

"Murph and I are good friends. That won't change." He walked towards the door.

"Jax?" the lieutenant called out. "You would have made one hell of a good detective."

He threw his hand up in a wave and left. He said goodbye to Alma on his way out, but before he reached the main office, Tim stood there waiting for him, looking as tired and disheveled as he felt.

"Jax, what's going on?"

"We need to talk, Murph. C'mon, I'll buy you a cup of coffee."

Tim winced and turned away from him for a second. "Aw, crap, you quit, didn't you?

"What makes you say that?" Jax asked.

"Because you always make me buy the coffee."

Jax chuckled as he threw his arm around Tim's shoulder and the two of them walked through the main office together. "Do me a favor, Murph. Grab the stuff from my desk later. I don't want to be here when the rest of the department finds out. A lot of these clowns will be glad to see me go."

"Well, I'm not happy about it at all."

"That's good because I plan on coming over to your place pretty often for Carla's home-cooked meals. Heck, I'll have time on my hands now. Maybe she can teach me how to cook. I've been wanting to learn, and it'll save me some money. I could even watch Lizzie and Petey for a couple of hours while you and Carla go out on the town once in a while. See? Some good will come of this."

They climbed down the stairs to the front door. "Jesus, I bet they team me up with Collins and Moriarty now," Tim complained. "Those two are a couple of saps, just like you said."

"Stan isn't so bad, but Butch is missing more than a few cards in his deck." When they got outside, a newsboy walked by with a satchel of morning papers. "Hey, kid!" Jax called to him. "Can I get one of those?" He handed the boy a nickel. "Thanks."

Tim led the way to his patrol car parked on the side of the road. "You never buy the newspaper."

"I need to start looking for a new job in the want ads."

Tim grumbled under his breath and got into the car. "Well, at least I get to do all the driving from now on."

"I told you, Murph. I get car sick riding in the passenger seat."

"I don't buy that fairy tale for one second." Tim started the car and headed down the road. "Let's stop for coffee at Roxy's Diner over in Brooklyn near our apartments. I want to swing by and see Carla and the kids for a minute afterward. Why don't you come with me, then I'll drop you off at your place?"

"Aren't you on duty?"

"I don't care. Let them fire me."

Jax laughed. "Sure, you wait until I leave the force to turn into a rebel." He unfolded the newspaper and was prepared to pass right by the front page. He figured all the details about the bank shooting would consume the headlines. Instead, it focused on a different burglary. "Get a load of this, Murph. A couple of crooks robbed Henri Bendel's department store in Greenwich last night. No one was hurt, but they got away with a bundle."

"Bendel's is that ritzy store famous for their brown and white striped hat boxes and bags."

Jax raised a brow. "And you know this because..."

"Carla told me!" Tim snapped back. "She and her mother went window-shopping there once. Carla said some of their hats cost over a hundred bucks."

"That explains how the crooks made off with thousands of dollars' worth of merchandise."

"The store is in the Sixth Precinct district, isn't it?" Tim asked.

"Yeah, lucky for us."

Tim glanced over at him. "Lucky for me, you mean."

"Oh, yeah, right." They both fell silent for a few minutes. "I can't stay on the force, Murph."

"Yeah, I know, Jax. It just stinks, that's all."

3

Tramp

With his hands tucked in his overcoat pockets and the newspaper under his arm, Jax leaned against the brick building directly across the street from the Chase National Bank on the Lower East Side. Hours ago, Tim had dropped him off at his apartment after a quick visit with Carla and the kids, but within thirty seconds, the walls seemed to close in on him. So he left his apartment and just rode around on the subway until he ended up here.

'After the event, even a fool is wise.' It was a quote by Homer that Jax remembered reading, and it suited yesterday's disaster perfectly. At the orphanage where he grew up, Sister Rosemary knew his reading skills exceeded the other children, so she would sneak into Father Patrick's private library and bring him more advanced books to read, like *War and Peace* by Leo Tolstoy, and Homer's poems. Jax also possessed an exceptional memory, but that had proven to be more of a curse than a blessing.

Over and over again he replayed yesterday's events in his mind, and he kept thinking about the basement window. As soon as that pup had drawn his attention to it, in a flash he'd formed a mental image of every step he needed to take after entering the bank, right up to how he intended to disarm the robbers. He'd even pegged his plan as having a ninety percent chance of success.

Yet, what got in the way was that last questionable ten percent, along with the absolute guarantee he'd lose his job.

Something touched his foot, and he glanced down. The little black and tan ball of fur was sitting beside him, facing the bank with his front paw propped on Jax's leather boot. "Hey, pal. I was just thinking about you. I never had a chance to thank you for your help yesterday." Jax stared at the bank again. "It didn't end well, though. I should have followed your lead."

The pup barked once, then the two of them quietly remained in the same position for another good thirty minutes.

Jax looked down at the puppy again. "I need to get something to eat. Do you like pretzels?"

The pup popped up on his feet, wagging his tail.

"C'mon. We'll get a couple of them across the street at Ratner's. I owe you that much. Then, I need to go home, and you should, too."

For the next hour, Jax and the pup sat on the sidewalk in front of the deli under the awning, eating their treats and watching the passersby, although Jax kept glancing at the bank on the corner. Finally, he got up, said goodbye to the puppy, and headed down the sidewalk to the subway entrance a few blocks away.

But the puppy proudly strutted along beside him.

Jax stopped walking. "Okay, hold on, pal. This is where we part ways. I'm sure we'll run into each other again." He continued on, but the puppy kept walking with him. When Jax reached the stairwell to the subway, he sighed and bent down to pet him. "See you later, buddy. Now, stay put."

Jax climbed down the stairs and caught the subway. After he got home, Tim called to see how he was doing and tried to convince him to come over for dinner. Jax put him off by telling him that he'd made other plans. Tim didn't buy it, but he didn't argue with him either. Jax said he'd talk to him tomorrow. Then, he just wandered around his apartment, not knowing what to do with himself.

Finally, he went into the other room, but like the previous night, he tried sleeping in his bed, moved to the couch, and ended up standing in front of his living room window until morning. He knew there wasn't a damn thing he could do to change what had happened, but he couldn't get past the anger, heartache, and frustration of it, or the memory of the part he played in it.

Yet, as the skies brightened the next morning, the storm clouds cleared away, and the sunrise put on a magnificent show as though shouting to the world, *it's a new day and a new beginning.*

Jax remained there a while longer, then he sat down at the kitchen table with a cup of strong coffee, yesterday's newspaper, and a pencil to circle any jobs that suited him. All too quickly, he grew discouraged as he skimmed through multiple listings for maids, dressmakers, telephone operators, and factory workers. The only positions that even remotely interested him were for cooks at various restaurants from high-end hotels to rinky-dink breakfast joints and the busy automat in Times Square. But his cooking experience was limited to slapping together a bologna sandwich, boiling a couple of eggs in a pot for ten minutes, and brewing his own beer.

Disgruntled, he turned the page, and there it was, like a sign from above.

'Become a Gourmet Cook before Christmas: Renowned French Chef Dupuis is offering five two-hour classes at the Hotel Lafayette on the corner of University Place and East Ninth Street...'

Jax read further down and found out the first class started this afternoon at two o'clock, and there were only a couple of spots open. It also cost five dollars, which was nothing to scoff at. He'd saved a little money for emergencies, but without any income, he didn't want to cut himself short.

"What the heck." He circled the telephone number, then turned back to the front page to read the article about the department store robbery.

By ten o'clock, Jax had washed up and dressed in his brown tweed suit and paisley bowtie with a white handkerchief tucked into the breast pocket of his jacket. He called the hotel to reserve his place in the cooking class and left his apartment to catch the subway. As he locked the door, he saw Lucinda, the tall blonde who lived down the hall, leaving her apartment. He was in no mood to chitchat with her, so he tried to make a quick exit, but she called out to him.

"Officer Diamond, wait up!"

He rolled his eyes and slowed his pace. "Good morning, Lucinda."

"You're looking dapper this morning." She boldly slipped her arm around his and continued walking. "I've never seen you out of uniform. Do you have the day off?"

He pressed his index finger over his mouth. "Shh, I'm undercover today."

She giggled. "Ooh, how exciting. My lips are sealed."

He held the front door open for her. "You're out and about early this morning."

"Trudy and I made gobs of tips last night at the club, so we're spending the day shopping in Manhattan. Too bad you're working. The three of us could have a swell time."

"My loss," he laughed. "Well, I'm heading in the other direction. I'll see you later, Lucinda."

She blew him a kiss. "Toodle-oo!"

Slowly, he walked down the sidewalk, glimpsing behind him until Lucinda disappeared around the corner. Then he quickly retraced his steps. When he reached DeKalb Street, he caught sight of her climbing down the stairs to the subway station. So, he decided to take a trolley to Greenwich Village to avoid running into her again.

After he turned down Duffield Street, he heard the trolley bells and waited by the road. Only a handful of people were on board, so he had a seat all to himself. As he looked out the window, his mind overflowed with a hundred thoughts and questions, which always happened when he and Tim were working on a case. Even though he'd quit the force, right now was no different.

The robbery at Bendel's department store bugged him, which is why he wanted to scout the place out this morning. Posing as a curious, swanky shopper, he knew he could find out plenty from the salesclerks and even check out the building itself. According to the newspaper article, there was no sign of forced entry into the store, at least not at the time of publication. So, the robbery was either an inside job or the police missed something.

But all those thoughts suddenly vanished. The trolley had turned onto Allen Street, heading north now, and stopped at the intersection at Delancey Street. Instinctively, Jax glanced down the road and regretted it. He saw the Chase National Bank two short blocks away, and his mind became cluttered with a whole pile of depressing thoughts. Again, he couldn't shake them, not until they had traveled a couple miles away, and the trolley approached his destination on East Ninth Street.

While staring out the window, he suddenly did a double take. Then he practically wrenched his neck watching that scruffy little puppy strut down the sidewalk, skillfully weaving in and out of the foot traffic. As soon as the trolley stopped in front of Bendel's department store, Jax hurriedly got off and searched back through the crowd they'd just passed, looking for the little tramp, yet he didn't see hide nor hair of him.

Finally, he gave up and headed for the store. Before he entered, a Salvation Army volunteer stood out front, ringing her bell for donations. He reached into his pocket and tossed a nickel into the red kettle.

Inside the store, Jax's blue eyes grew wide as he stood there, glancing around in utter amazement. In all his life, he'd never seen anything like this. Of course, the minimal amount of shopping he'd done was always in the nickel and dime stores like Woolworths. Even working on the police force, he'd merely dealt with two-bit shoplifters and thieves in those types of stores. So, he couldn't help but become mesmerized by the elaborate display of Christmas decorations.

Everywhere he looked, there were ornamental Christmas trees and wreaths. Ropes of garland had been strung across the entire store, and stuffed elves and reindeer dangled from the twelve-foot ceilings along with dozens of what he assumed were empty boxes wrapped in flashy, colorful paper, adding to the holiday cheer. Even the mammoth chandelier in the center flaunted large red velvet bows. The jam-packed store also roared with laughter and chatter, drowning out the children's chorus singing Christmas tunes somewhere on the main floor.

Jax spotted two men standing at attention on either side of the front doors with their hands clasped in front of them. He pegged them as hired watchmen and decided to strike up a conversation with the most amicable one, who nodded to the customers as they entered.

He strolled over to the man. "Pardon me, but would you kindly direct me to the men's department? I'm from out of town, and my brother said your store carries the highest quality suits."

"Merry Christmas, sir," the man replied. "The menswear is on the second floor. The elevator is located down this aisle. If you prefer taking the stairs, they're just beyond it."

"Thank you." Jax tipped his hat and walked away a few steps, but he deliberately halted and turned to the man again. "My brother also mentioned your store was burglarized the other night. Did they ever find the culprits?"

"Not to my knowledge, sir. That's the reason for extra security. It occurred after hours, so no need to worry."

"Well, that's a relief. It's happening more and more everywhere, even in Philadelphia. That's where I'm from. Did they get away with a significant amount of merchandise? I'm a businessman, myself, and any theft can put a painful dent in the profits."

"They're still going through their inventory to see if anything else is missing, but right now, it looks like they just cleaned out the toy department on the third floor."

"They stole toys?"

"Yes, sir."

"Isn't that odd? This is a very upscale department store. You would think they would have stolen more valuable items."

"Mister Bendel is pretty upset. I guess the store has plenty of insurance to cover things like furs and jewelry, but not children's toys. Another shipment is expected today, but the third floor is roped off temporarily. They moved their winter display with Santa Claus to the back of the main floor."

"How did those scoundrels break in?"

"That's the trouble. The police couldn't find any sign of forced entry."

"You don't think an employee was involved, do you? That happened a couple of years ago at Wanamaker's Department Store where I live."

"Right now, it's anyone's guess. The owner hired us from an outside security company to monitor both the customers and the employees."

"Good to know. It was nice chatting with you." Jax tipped his hat to him again and walked down the aisle towards the stairway to the second floor.

He'd gotten an earful from the security guard, but he wanted to make it look good, so he stopped at the bottom of the stairway to listen to the group of children singing Christmas carols. Just beyond them, Jax noticed a long line of other children with their parents leading into another room. Out of curiosity, he moved closer and smiled when he saw the attraction.

Santa Claus sat in a large high-back chair against the far wall beside a beautifully decorated Christmas tree. Stacks of wrapped presents surrounded him, two elves flanked his chair, and a row of colorful wooden nutcrackers lined the shelf behind him, similar to the one that had been given to Jax.

A young boy sat on Santa's lap, excitedly telling him all the things he wanted for Christmas. When he was done, he kissed Santa on the cheek and joined his mother, waiting for him.

Jax took the scene in for a minute, then he lost his grin. He'd never been keen on the Christmas holidays, stemming from his own childhood, but after what happened this week, he knew the Christmas holidays would forever remind him of the little boy at the bank who would never enjoy another one again. He shook his head to get rid of those wretched thoughts and ventured upstairs to the second floor.

He walked through the men's department, pretending to be looking for a new suit. While shuffling through one of the racks, he nearly choked when he saw the price tag. He finally headed back to the stairway and noticed a couple of watchmen on this floor, too, but he didn't want to appear too inquisitive by questioning them. He was also anxious to get a look at the exterior of the building.

Outside, Jax walked around to the back of the building and saw the loading docks. There weren't any workers in sight, so he casually wandered down the drive, staying close to the building until he reached the doorway. The brass door lever looked new, and it was locked securely. He inspected the rest of the structure, yet he didn't see any scrapes or knicks indicating it had been forced open.

Then he poked the tip of his index finger into a small circular opening in the bottom corner of the door window, just above the door handle.

4

Ninette

Jax walked down East Ninth Street again, thinking about that small hole in the back door window. He had plenty of time to kill before his cooking class started at the Hotel Lafayette just up the road. Since Greenwich Village was known for its wide variety of small shops, he decided to wander around for a while and grab some lunch at one of the cafés.

For over an hour, he strolled down the sidewalk with his hands tucked in his overcoat pockets. Every once in a while, he stopped to admire one of the window displays, and he slowed his pace as he passed a bakery, relishing in the mouth-watering fragrance of freshly baked cinnamon rolls. He waited on the corner with a crowd of people until the traffic allowed them to cross the street. On the other side, he continued walking, but he stopped short just before an alleyway.

A boy wearing suspenders and knickers who looked about twelve or thirteen years old stood with his back tightly pressed against the brick wall as though hiding from someone. His freckled face was beet red, and he kept cussing at something on the ground by his feet. As soon as a group of people passed by, Jax saw what was infuriating him.

That scruffy little tramp had grabbed the kid's argyle sock between his teeth, and he refused to let go of it. Jax snickered as he watched them.

"Get out of here!" the kid yelled at the puppy. "Let me go!"

But the little rascal growled and snarled and, with his back paws planted firmly on the ground, he tugged on the kid's sock with all his might.

A man came running down the sidewalk. "Someone stop him! He stole my wallet!"

The kid heard the man's voice and panicked. He shoved the puppy away and darted out of the alley, but Jax stuck his foot out as the boy rushed by him. The kid tripped and nosedived onto the sidewalk with the wallet flying out of his hands. Before the owner could reach them, the boy had scrambled to his feet and skedaddled down the road.

The puppy retrieved the wallet and proudly sat down beside him.

Jax laughed his head off. "Good boy."

The man slowed his pace. "Where did that kid go?"

"He's long gone," Jax told him, and he pointed at the puppy. "But this little guy saved the day."

The man started chuckling. "Well, I'll be. Thanks, pooch." He reached down and retrieved the wallet from the puppy's mouth. "Here. Buy your partner a treat on me." The man handed him a dollar bill.

Jax tipped his hat to the man. "Have a good day, sir." Then, he lifted his brow and threw the puppy a look of surprise. "I guess you're buying us lunch today. C'mon, *partner*." He smiled, and the two of them walked down the road.

They stopped at one of the food carts, and Jax ordered two hot dogs with bacon and cheese. He paid the man and found an empty wooden bench. He lifted the puppy up next to him, and they both enjoyed their lunch while watching the crowd of people walking by. Within minutes, two pretty young women stopped to pet the puppy, and they both gushed over him. Soon, a few other women did the same, and Jax sat back smiling, watching the puppy gobble up all the attention.

"You're such a ham," he whispered. Another group of women shoppers approached them, squealing with excitement, and it went on from there as they sat together, watching the bustling crowds.

Jax looked at his watch again. "I need to get to class soon, and I hate leaving you here by yourself. Let's see if any of the store owners know where you live."

They walked back down the street and every so often, Jax poked his head inside a few stores. He stopped at a smoke shop, a shoe store, and a candy store, and asked the owners and clerks about the puppy. They all either shrugged their shoulders, simply commented on how cute he was, or replied they didn't know who he belonged to. He also asked the street vendors along the way and received the same answers.

Jax was running out of time, so he stopped at one more store. He opened the door to the barbershop. The owner was busy giving one of his customers a shave, and two other men were waiting. "Excuse me. Would any of you fine gentlemen know where this little guy lives?"

The barber and the two men waiting glanced over and shook their heads. Then, the man in the swivel chair sat upright and pulled the hot cloth off his face. "That looks like the dog someone dumped off in the alley next to my brother's butcher shop on Delancey a few weeks ago."

Jax looked at the puppy and frowned. "That's where I first saw him. Poor little guy. He can't be much older than a couple of months. He wandered pretty far from home. Any chance you can take him back there?"

"Sorry. I need to get to work, and I don't clock out until ten tonight."

"Okay, thanks." Jax left the shop and bent down to pet the puppy. "At least we know where you live. Look, I've got some silly cooking class to go to right now. If you want to hang around here for a couple of hours, I'll take you back home on the subway when I'm done. I still have some of your reward money left."

Jax headed for the hotel and, as he expected, the puppy walked along with him. When he reached the front door, he repeated what he'd said to the puppy and went inside.

He approached the man behind the front desk. "Good afternoon. I signed up for that cooking class. Could you tell me where it's being held?"

The man grinned at him with delight. "Certainly. It is right up the hall. I will escort you there. Follow me, sir."

"Thank you," Jax replied. "I believe there's a five-dollar charge?"

"Yes. You can pay the chef." He stopped in front of the second door, still smiling. "I think you will find yourself pleasantly surprised."

As soon as the man opened the door for him, Jax wasn't sure what he felt. Eight women in all different sizes, shapes, and hair color wearing white bibbed aprons stood all lined up in a row behind a long counter, facing him.

He whispered to the desk clerk, "You're pulling my leg, right?"

The man chuckled. "No, sir. Enjoy the class."

Jax desperately wanted to make a quick exit, too, but another woman approached him. She was dressed in a white chef's coat and hat, red neckerchief, and slim black skirt. And she was no bug-eyed Betty.

"You must be Jax Diamond," she said with a thick French accent. "I was quite pleased to see your name on the list. I wish more of your *regular joes*, as you say, would show such an interest. I am Chef Ninette Dupuis."

He handed her the five-dollar bill, and she told him to take his place behind the counter. Feeling like a real ass, he hung his overcoat on one of the wall hooks, smiled at the others, and made his way behind the counter.

"Heck, nothing ventured, nothing gained. Good afternoon, ladies!" They all greeted him and budged down a bit to give him more room at the end. The short little redhead beside him introduced herself as Nancy and offered to help him tie the bibbed apron around his waist. Pretty soon, all the women were leaning forward, introducing themselves to him.

Ninette came forward. "Ladies...and gentleman, eyes up front, s'il vous plaît. If you please. You have each been supplied with your own single-burner alcohol stove and a frying pan, along with the necessary ingredients and tools that you will need. Since this is our first class, we will begin by making a simple crepe. They are similar to a thin, flat pancake, which can then be stuffed with a wide variety of fillings to make everything from delicious hors d'oeuvres to sumptuous gourmet meals to sweet and rich desserts."

For the next two hours, Ninette walked them through the proper steps, then strolled about the room, both correcting and praising them. Jax and the ladies concentrated on the task at hand, mixing, pouring, and cooking, and for most of them, burning the first few. Yet, by the end of the class, they all stood there proudly with their own small stack of perfect crepes in front of them.

"It seems our time is up," Ninette announced. "You have all done very well, and I am quite impressed. Feel free to take your crepes home in those small bags. Here is a list of a variety of fillings to turn them into a divine dinner, hors d'oeuvres, or dessert. Simply wrap your crepes around the filling and serve." She gave them each a copy of the list. "At our next class tomorrow, we will make hollandaise sauce, and discuss the difference between hollandaise and béarnaise sauce, so you will have two deliciously rich sauces to add to a variety of main dishes. Have a good evening."

They all took their aprons off, and the women started chatting excitedly as they packed up their crepes. Jax tossed his into a bag and followed along behind the others. They all grabbed their coats and headed out the door.

"Jax?" Ninette called to him. "Could I speak with you for a moment?"

He heard a few of the women giggle as they left. "Sure," he replied.

He waited while Ninette removed her chef's hat and tossed her short black curls around. She slipped her coat off next, and she was wearing a rather revealing lacey black blouse. After she laid the coat carefully over the back of the chair beside her, she faced him.

"Already, I can see you are going to be my star pupil, Jax. You are a quick learner, no? I do wonder what coerced you into taking this class. Surely, you have a wife at home who cooks your meals for you."

He looked into her eyes, which were as black as her hair. "I thought it would be fun."

She laughed. "Ah, vous cherchez une femme."

He smiled at her glib comment that he was looking for a wife. "Non, je veux apprendre à cuisiner."

Her small mouth dropped open. "You speak French?"

"A little, and I'm not looking for a wife. I just want to learn how to cook." She stepped toward him, staring at him a little too provocatively, and he cleared his throat. "Well, I should be going. It was great meeting you, Chef Dupuis. I'll see you in class tomorrow."

She walked him to the door. "I look forward to it, Jax."

He left the hotel carrying his bag of crepes and as soon as he was outside, he loosened his bowtie as things had gotten a little heated in there. With everything else going on, he certainly didn't need to complicate it by getting romantically involved with his teacher.

He remembered the puppy and looked all around for him. It was going on four-thirty, and although he only half-expected the little guy to be waiting outside the hotel after such a long time, he worried about him finding his way home.

Yet, there was nothing he could do about it now, so he made his way to the subway station on the next corner. He climbed down the stairs, paid his nickel, and waited for the train. As soon as it pulled up and stopped, Jax waited for the doors to open, then he hopped on.

"Hey, Mister!" someone yelled. "You forgot your dog!"

Jax spun around and saw the little scruff ball sitting on the platform, staring at him.

He got off the train, laughing. He waved his thanks to the kid, picked the little guy up, and boarded the subway again. "Let's get you home."

When they reached Delancey Street, Jax carried the puppy off the train and up the flight of stairs. Then he set him on the ground. He spotted the butcher shop across the street from Ratner's. They crossed the road when it was clear of traffic and walked down the sidewalk. As soon as they reached the store, Jax bent down.

"You're home and safe now. I'll come back to see how you're doing tomorrow, okay?" He patted the puppy on the head and walked back down the sidewalk.

But the puppy followed him.

Jax looked down. "You're not going to make this easy, are you? I guess that's my fault. C'mon." They headed back to the butcher shop. Jax noticed a dark-haired, chubby man wearing a heavily stained apron in the alley just before it. The man was holding a garden hose and rinsing his hands and arms. "Excuse me!" Jax called out. "Are you the owner of the butcher shop?"

The man glanced over, grinning. "Yes, I am. How can I help you, sir?"

"I found your puppy in Greenwich Village and..."

The butcher got one look at the puppy and flew into a rage. "Get that filthy varmint out of here!" He pointed the hose at the puppy, turned up the nozzle, and a powerful gush of water blasted out, striking the puppy, who raced away.

"Hey, cut that out!" Jax shouted at him.

The man turned the water off, threw the hose on the ground, and stomped towards him with his arms flailing. "I've been trying to get rid of that damn dog for weeks! He keeps knocking over my trash cans! Get out of here! Both of you!"

Jax looked at the four-foot-tall cans lined up against the wall, then he glared at the man. Without another word, he marched over, gave the first trash can a good, swift kick, and all four of them went tumbling to the ground, dumping out all the trash and making a bloody mess.

"Next time, pick on someone your own size!" Jax stormed away, found the soaking puppy waiting for him around the corner, picked him up, and carried him back to the subway.

5

Welcome Home

Jax had calmed down by the time he got to his apartment. He'd also dried the puppy off with his jacket, and he set him on the floor just inside the doorway. "This is where I live. I admit the place isn't much, but it's probably better than where you've been sleeping. I don't have a lot of food, but..."

The puppy sprinted into the kitchen.

"I'll take that as a yes to a bologna and cheese sandwich," Jax laughed. He followed the puppy and looked at the bag of crepes in his hand. "Why not?"

He stuffed two of the crepes with bologna and a slice of cheese, folded them up, and cut one of them into little pieces. Then, he sat down at the table, set the puppy's plate on the floor, and they both enjoyed their dinner.

As soon as they were finished, the puppy disappeared into the living room.

Jax found him standing by the back door, wagging his tail. "You want to leave already? I figured you'd at least want to stay the night."

The puppy barked at the door, so Jax reluctantly opened it, and the puppy scampered outside.

"I guess I can't blame you," Jax said sullenly. "Sorry, little guy."

He closed the door and plopped down on the couch, feeling even more depressed about his life than before. He'd witnessed a horrible crime, quit a job he loved, and blew five dollars on a dumb cooking class. Now, it was only a matter of a few weeks before he was dead broke. He heaved another sigh and shook his head in disgust.

But he suddenly heard scratching at the back door. He waited a minute, then he got up and opened it. The puppy pranced inside like he owned the joint. He propped his paws up on the couch and looked over at Jax for a little help.

He laughed. "Oh, you had to do your business, huh?" He lifted the puppy onto the couch and watched him circle around, pawing at the material before he finally curled up into a ball. Jax sat down beside him. "If you decide you want to make this your home, we're going to have to rig up a revolving door for you."

He leaned back while petting the puppy. "You know...you and I have a lot in common. After I was born, I was dumped off like a bag of beans, too. My parents, or whoever it was, never even had the courtesy of leaving a note as to my real name or where I came from. They just stuck that dang jack of diamonds playing card at the bottom of my basket. That's how I got my name." He noticed the puppy was sound asleep. "We don't know your name either, but we'll figure it out tomorrow."

Saturday, December 17

Jax groaned and folded his pillow over his head, trying to drown out all the racket. Finally, he opened one eye, then they both flew open when he found himself staring at the rear end and wagging tail of the barking puppy. "What the heck..."

He bolted upright in bed and heard someone pounding on his front door. He shoved the covers off and got up. As soon as he set the puppy on the floor, the little scruff ball raced into the other room, yapping away. Jax heard a clunk, then a thud, and figured the puppy had run into the small table by the sofa.

"Hang on, Murph! I'm coming!" After he threw a pair of trousers on, he went into the other room, swung the door open, and Tim stood there in uniform. "Are you trying to wake everybody up in the building? It's only eight o'clock in the morning."

"We need to talk, Jax," Tim said, but the puppy started growling. Both Jax and Tim slowly lowered their heads and saw that he'd grabbed hold of Tim's shoelace and was tugging on it. "Isn't that the puppy who was at the bank the other day?" Tim asked. "What the heck is he doing here?"

"It's a long story." Jax spun around and headed into the kitchen to make some coffee. "Isn't it Saturday? Why are you in uniform?"

The puppy dropped the shoelace and followed him.

After Tim tied his shoe, he went over and leaned against the kitchen doorway with his arms folded in front of him. "If you'd answer my phone calls, you'd know why."

Jax reached into the icebox, then he started chopping up a piece of bologna and a hard-boiled egg on a plate. "Well, you're here now. Why don't you tell me?"

"Lieutenant Simmons called me into the office this morning. He said a store owner on Delancey Street had notified the police that he wanted to press vandalism charges against someone fitting your description. The lieutenant told me to go to the butcher shop and check it out."

Jax put the plate on the floor. "And did you?"

"I'm guessing the puppy had something to do with it?" When Jax didn't respond, Tim added, "I explained to the owner that you were the first officer on the scene at the bank robbery the other day. He felt bad and dropped the charges."

"I should be filing charges against him," Jax stated as poured two cups of coffee and motioned for Tim to sit down at the kitchen table with him. He opened the paper bag on the table and moved the butter dish closer. "Want a crepe?" He pulled two of them out and started spreading butter on them.

"Where the heck did you get crepes?"

"I made them." Jax handed him one.

Tim stared at it like it was poison. "You made these?"

"Yeah, I had my first cooking class yesterday." He took a bite. "Hmm, they're pretty good."

Tim tried it and nodded his approval. "Not bad. So, where are these classes?"

"At a hotel in Greenwich Village. While I was over that way, I decided to snoop around Bendel's department store, where that robbery took place the other night."

"Jax..."

He threw his hand up in the air. "I know, *Officer Murphy*. I'm not on the police force anymore. I just went there out of curiosity. Murph, you and Carla need to take the kids to that place. The entire store is decorated fancier than a Christmas tree, and there was a line a mile long of kids waiting to sit on Santa's lap. He looked like the real deal, too. I swear his beard was genuine, and he sounded just as jolly as you'd think he would."

"Henri Bendel can afford to hire the real Santa. What did you find out about the robbery?"

"Get this. A security guard told me that the crooks stole all their toys. The entire department was cleaned out."

Tim crinkled his brows. "Why would they steal toys?"

"I don't know. The guard said they were still looking through their inventory for anything else missing, but so far, only the toys were stolen. He worked for an outside security company and was instructed to monitor the employees and the customers since there was no sign of forced entry."

Tim glared at him when he stopped talking and sipped his coffee. "What else did you find out? You're keeping something from me."

Jax grinned. "First, why don't you tell me the *real* reason you stopped by?"

Tim burst out laughing. "I can't pull the wool over your eyes, can I? There were two more heists last night. That's why the lieutenant wanted me to work today."

Jax set his crepe down on the table. "Where?"

"Macy's in Manhattan and that big, gaudy department store right here in Brooklyn on the corner of Fulton and Hoyt Streets."

"Abraham & Straus? Whew, that store is the crème de la crème for all those swanky socialites who live in Upper Manhattan."

"Showing off your French again?" Tim asked.

"You don't know the half of it. Does it look like the same crooks?"

"After hours, no sign of entry, and again, they stole a bundle, but I don't know what merchandise they got away with," Tim told him.

"Was anyone hurt?" Jax asked.

"A couple of night guards at both stores were knocked out, but they'll be fine. None of them saw it coming, so they couldn't identify the thieves. All three precincts have joined forces in the investigation. So far, they haven't asked for our help, but the lieutenant wants to be prepared in case they do."

"They will. Robbing three major department stores is a pretty gutsy move. Those crooks aren't done yet. I just can't figure out why they targeted the toy department at Bendel's."

"Well, it is Christmastime, and toys are the most popular commodity right now."

"I guess..."

Tim waited for a second. "Okay, your turn."

"It may be nothing, Murph, but after I left Bendel's, I wandered around to the loading docks in the back of the store. I couldn't find any sign of forced entry either, but there was a small, clean hole in the bottom corner of the door window."

"What do you make of that?"

"I'm not sure yet. I'd like to take a look around the other two stores. I'll start with Abraham & Straus since it's the closest."

"Keep me posted and, for crying out loud, be careful. We've stepped on a few toes in all three precincts, and I'm sure you don't have many get-out-of-jail-free cards left."

"I'll be careful. So, did Captain Ryan team you up with the Bobbsey twins?"

Tim snickered. "Not yet. I don't think Stan and Butch want to ride with me any more than I want to ride with them, but it's probably only a matter of time. Right now, I'm training Jeffrey MacDougal. He's waiting in the patrol car outside."

"Oh, cripes. Your head's going to swell even bigger with that yes-man kissing your feet all the time."

"That sounds a hell of a lot better than working with someone who always gives me a hard time like my last partner." Tim tipped his head back and pointed into the living room. "Hey Jax, your puppy is waiting by the back door."

He jumped out of his chair. "C'mon, you've got to see this." He hurried into the other room with Tim following along and as soon as he opened the back door, the puppy dashed outside. "He'll do his business and head right back." They waited a minute and a half. "Here he comes. Now watch what he does."

The puppy pranced inside, headed for the couch, lifted his front paws on it, and looked over at them. Jax quickly picked him up and set him on the cushions. The puppy dug around in circles and curled up to go to sleep.

"Hold on," Jax said as he grabbed the sock lying on the floor and tied a knot in it. "He untied your shoelace, but he's got a better trick." Jax set the knotted sock in front of the puppy. "Watch this."

The puppy spotted it and moved closer. He placed a paw on one end of the sock, then started tugging on the knot with his teeth, slowly pulling the other end through using his other paw. It took him a minute, and after the knot pulled free, he curled up and fell asleep.

"Isn't he smart?" Jax folded his arms in front of him, smiling proudly. "He doesn't chew anything. He just tugs at stuff. He sleeps a lot, too."

Tim grinned. "Puppies do when they're content."

"Yeah, I slept pretty soundly myself last night. It's been a while."

"Two peas in a pod," Tim laughed. "Well, Jax, it looks like you found your ace."

His face lit up. "Ace! That's the perfect name for him." He looked at the puppy again. "The highest card in the deck. Thanks, Murph."

"I'd better get back to work," Tim said, still chuckling. "What do you two have planned for today outside of snooping around at the department stores?"

"First thing I have to do is cut a hole in the bottom of my back door and rig up some sort of flap so Ace can come and go as he pleases."

Tim rolled his eyes. "Oh, that'll go over swell with your landlord. Why don't you bring the little guy over for dinner tonight? Carla and Lizzie will love meeting him."

After Tim left, Jax noticed the nutcracker had fallen on the floor when Ace ran into the end table earlier. At first glance, the statue looked busted, but he picked it up and saw that a small section on the back of it had sprung open, like a secret compartment. Something was tucked inside. He couldn't squeeze his fingers through the opening, so he tipped the statue sideways.

A clay poker chip or marker dropped into his hand. It was painted black and white with four black squares evenly placed near the outer edge, each one holding an imprint of a white heart, diamond, spade, and club. Yet, a large black star filled the center. He wondered what the star signified, then placed the nutcracker back on the table and took the chip with him into the kitchen.

6

A Paris Affair

Jax knew the two of them looked like the comic strip characters Mutt and Jeff walking down the road together with his height at six foot three and the puppy standing no taller than nine inches from the top of his head to the ground. Yet again, every passerby stopped to shower Ace with all kinds of compliments and attention, and he lapped it all up.

"It's like strolling along the Coney Island boardwalk with a Broadway star," Jax quipped. "But that could work in our favor. The department store is up ahead, and I have a feeling that despite their store policy, we'll both be welcome. Let me carry you inside, and we'll give it a shot."

While his tactic worked, Jax wasn't at all prepared for what he found when they entered Abraham & Straus, even after seeing Bendel's store yesterday. This department store was at least three times bigger. The main corridor was set up like a beautiful, outdoor courtyard with thirty-foot-high ceilings which exposed three upper levels and led straight up to the mammoth circular skylight overhead. Each department on the main floor had its own window display and entrance off the corridor. The entire place simply burst with colorful decorations along with an organist playing Christmas tunes in the backdrop, and there was a full crowd of shoppers.

"We're way out of our league in here, Ace," he whispered. "I'd better keep carrying you, or you'll get trampled on."

They slowly wandered down the main corridor, zigzagging through the throngs of people. As they went, Jax kept a lookout for anyone who appeared to be part of the store's security staff. He was anxious to learn more about the burglary last night, especially finding out exactly what merchandise was stolen.

Yet, unlike Bendel's, he didn't see any guards standing by the front doors or anywhere else in view, which he found curious. So, he pretended to be a customer and stopped in a few of the departments to chat with the salesclerks about the robberies, but as soon as he gently broached the subject, they all clammed up.

One thing he found rather interesting. After leaving the perfume counter, he paused to watch the clerk wrap a rubber band around a thick stack of cash. Then, she put it into the bottom opening of a tall, wide cylinder that reached up to the ceiling and used a pulley to send the money upstairs. It was a huge wad of dough, which meant they kept a vault here somewhere. He had noticed those cylinders scattered inside a few of the departments and thought they were merely decorative pillars.

When they reached the bronze elevator on the left just before the end of the corridor, a young attendant stood in front of it wearing a light gray uniform, matching bellhop cap, and white gloves.

"Going up, sir?" he asked. "The women's and men's departments are on the second floor, children's clothing and our Santa Kingdom are on the third floor, and the Paris Fashion Show is in progress on the fourth floor. The fifth floor is furniture and appliances."

Jax grinned at Ace and replied, "I think we'll check out the fourth floor, thanks." They stepped inside.

After Jax turned around, he noticed a man dressed in a black suit standing in front of the window display only a few feet away. His homburg hat was tipped low over his brows, and as the elevator doors closed, the man blatantly glanced over at them.

"What's your puppy's name?" the attendant asked.

"Ace," Jax replied.

And right on cue, Ace barked.

The attendant laughed. "He knows his name."

"He's pretty smart," Jax boasted. "Say, I heard there was some kind of burglary here last night?"

"Yeah, Mister Straus called a mandatory meeting before we opened this morning. He was pretty upset, especially since he's part owner of Macy's, too, and both stores were robbed."

"I didn't know the stores had joint owners."

"Nathan Straus and his brother, Isidor, own Macy's. They partnered with Abraham in this store years ago. Unfortunately, Isidor and his wife died on the Titanic, but their son ended up marrying Abraham's daughter, so both stores are still run by all three families."

"Interesting. What type of merchandise did they steal?"

"We weren't given any details at the meeting, but my friend Mary works on the third floor. She said they had to rush around restocking the toy department early this morning since it was emptied. Luckily, another shipment had been delivered. They also stole a rare collection of porcelain dolls that had just arrived from Europe. That's got to be worth a fortune all on its own. The police were here and questioned all of us about where we were last night, like we were suspects or something."

"I'm sure that's just routine."

The elevator doors opened. Jax thanked the attendant and stepped onto the fourth floor, but he stood there for a second. There wasn't a customer anywhere in sight, and he only saw one salesclerk behind the cosmetic counter with her back to him.

Then he heard an announcer in the distance and set Ace down on the floor. "Let's get a look at this fashion show."

They walked down the side aisle until Jax saw the back section had been set up like a Broadway theater. Several rows of chairs stretched across the entire width of the store. A raised platform equipped with red velvet curtains consumed the back wall, and three bright spotlights were strategically shining on two fashion models gracefully strolling across the stage. It was a sold-out crowd, mostly upper-crust women, although a few high-hat gents were scattered throughout.

Jax leaned against the wall behind the last row to watch for a while, with Ace sitting at his feet. What he found puzzling was that despite the robbery last night, these models wore an array of designer outfits and an abundance of furs, along with layers of pricey necklaces, earrings, and bracelets. With all the wealth right here in this room, he knew the thieves must have had some ulterior motive for leaving all this behind.

His focus shifted to the four men standing at attention on the sidelines, two on the left side of the room and two on the right. He wondered if they were store employees, hired security, or personal bodyguards. With that last guess, he was curious if some dame of nobility was in attendance. Or a rich politician's wife.

Then he got his answer. A woman sitting dead center in the front row suddenly lifted her arm into the air and snapped her fingers. One of the men hurried over to her, bent down, and she whispered to him. The man looked over at Jax and headed in his direction.

Jax stretched his neck, trying to get a look at the woman, but she was sitting too far away. As the man approached them, Ace shot up on his stubby little feet and started snarling. "Settle down, tiger," Jax chuckled.

"Excuse me, sir," the man stated. "Mademoiselle Dupuis would like to invite you to join her."

Jax smirked. "Chef Dupuis?"

"Yes, sir."

Okay, that surprised him. Granted, the pageant focused on fashions from Paris, so it made perfect sense for her to attend. He also assumed she was fairly well-off, but he didn't realize she had so much clout. "Tell her thanks, maybe next time."

The man nodded. "Suit yourself."

Jax watched him walk back the way he came. After he gave Ninette his message, she turned around in her seat, and Jax tipped his hat to her. "C'mon, Ace." The two of them headed for the stairway, but no sooner did he reach the top step when someone called to him, and he turned around.

Ninette approached them. "Bonjour, Jax. I never expected to see you at a fashion show. You are a man of many wonders, aren't you?"

"Don't give me too much credit. I was talking with the elevator attendant and missed my floor."

She stepped closer, and her black-eyed stare unsettled him. "Perhaps after class this afternoon, you and I could go to a small café for a bite to eat? I would love to hear more about you and your diverse interests."

"Yeah, uh...sorry, we have dinner plans tonight."

"We?" She noticed Ace quietly sitting beside him. "Oh, you have a dog. Does he bite?"

Ace glanced up at Jax as though he wasn't humored by her remark at all.

"Well, we should go," Jax told her. "I'll see you in class later." He picked Ace up and headed down the stairs. "You could have been a little friendlier to her, Ace." He started chuckling. "Yeah, I guess I don't blame you. She comes across a little strong, doesn't she?"

As he walked through the corridor to the main entrance, he curiously looked up and studied the skylights. Outside, the two of them walked around the building so Jax could examine the windows. They approached a narrow drive that led to the store's loading docks, but he suddenly stopped. Nonchalantly, he looked around as though confused and trying to gather his bearings. In doing so, he glimpsed the person tailing them.

The man in the black suit and homburg hat who had watched them get on the elevator hung back a short distance away. Jax decided to alter their route and walked straight ahead, past the drive to the next street. They waited on the corner within the crowd to cross the road. When he was sure the fella was still following them, he and Ace continued down the sidewalk while Jax devised a plan to lose the guy.

"Okay, Ace, let's give him the slip." He picked Ace up again and carried him down the stairs to catch the subway.

As they waited for the train to arrive, Jax cuddled Ace and spoke to him softly, as though he were a small child. Yet, he was peeking over at their stalker who stood a distance away, facing the tracks.

"Don't get used to all this gooey attention," Jax whispered to Ace. "I'm just trying to keep an eye on that guy without him knowing."

When the train arrived and stopped in front of them, the doors opened. Jax waited a few seconds to let the passengers depart. Finally, he boarded the train, still holding Ace, but remained near the exit. The other man kept his sights on Jax and followed his movements exactly. He even stayed near the door at the other end of the car.

Jax listened closely. Once he heard the door click, he counted to three, then he swiftly stepped off the train just before the doors closed. The other man missed the signal, and Jax watched the train leave the station, knowing they'd successfully pulled a fast one on the guy.

"What a sap, Ace. That was almost too easy," he laughed. "Let's head back and take a look at those loading docks."

7

All About Toys?

Jax worried he'd be late for his cooking class and hurried to catch the next subway for Greenwich Village. He'd dropped Ace off at his apartment, left him plenty of food and water, and promised him that he'd only be a couple of hours. Luckily, Ace was exhausted from all the running around they'd done and fell fast asleep on the couch.

As soon as Jax reached the hotel, he waved to the front desk clerk and entered the classroom. He quickly hung his coat up, greeted the ladies behind the long counter, and took his place beside Nancy. "Where's our teacher?"

"I'm sure she'll be here soon," Nancy replied as she tied his apron for him. "Weren't those crepes we made delicious? I heated them up with sliced ham and melted cheddar cheese. Even my husband loved them, and he's a picky eater."

Judith leaned forward. "I filled some with strawberry jam for my children, and they were delicious."

"I thought they were great with just butter," Jax laughed.

"I don't think I've ever had hollandaise sauce before," Nancy said. "I'm dying to try it."

"My grandmother used to make it, but she never passed her recipe on to my mother," Mary said.

42

The door opened, and Ninette sauntered into the room dressed in her chef's uniform. "Good afternoon, class. I am happy to see you all here at your stations and eager to start. Once again, you have been equipped with the necessary ingredients and tools you will need to..." She stopped talking when she noticed Nancy whispering to Jax. "Excuse me, Nancy. Is there something you would like to share with the class?"

Nancy became flustered. "Oh, I'm sorry, Chef Dupuis. I was just asking Jax if he's ever had hollandaise sauce before. I apologize."

Ninette faced the class again. "First, I will explain the difference between hollandaise sauce and béarnaise sauce. They both include egg yolks, butter, and a dash of salt and pepper. Lemon juice is added to hollandaise for its smooth, yellowish texture. It is usually served over eggs, poached fish, and asparagus. Replace white wine vinegar for the lemon juice, add chopped shallots, and fresh herbs like tarragon and chervil, and you have made a superb béarnaise sauce. It will also appear pale yellow yet with flecks of green herbs. It is typically served with grilled meat and fish. To begin our hollandaise sauce, we must separate the egg yolks from the egg whites."

Ninette stepped over to the front of the counter to demonstrate the technique, then she instructed everyone to try it. Jax picked up an egg, cracked it, and half the yolk dropped into the bowl with the egg whites, along with a few pieces of eggshell. He looked over at Nancy, who had separated them perfectly.

"How did you do that, Nancy?"

"A lot of practice, Jax," she giggled. "Here, I'll show you."

But Ninette nudged between them. "Pay attention to your own tasks, Nancy. I will show Jax how to do it." She proceeded to help him with the second egg by intimately placing both of her hands over his. "You do not want to smash the egg. Just a gentle tap, then tip it upright and gently lift the top shell. See? That was perfect, Jax. Now drop the yolk into your pan and toss the shell away." She remained by his side. "Once everyone has separated the three egg yolks, turn your burners on low and whisk them vigorously." She held her dark gaze on Jax. "It is all about a gentle touch and impeccable timing."

Jax raised his brow yet remained silent.

By the end of the class, after several tries, they each stood in front of their saucepans with the same smooth, yellowish sauce. Ninette praised them and said the next class would be devoted to making lobster bisque using a roux to thicken the broth, which was a basic technique used in many creamed soups and gravies.

As they left the room, Ninette watched Jax as though she wanted to speak with him alone again, so he kept himself tucked within the group of women. Nancy chatted on, telling him that she couldn't wait for their next class. She had invited her entire family over for Christmas dinner, and she wanted to impress them all with a bowl of lobster bisque. As soon as they were outside, Jax quickly said goodbye to everyone and rushed off to catch the next subway since he was anxious to see if Ace was okay.

At five o'clock, Jax and Ace walked down the hall in Tim's apartment building, which was located right around the corner from his.

"I can't believe you slept the whole time I was gone, Ace," Jax told him. "That's probably good though because you're going to have a great time here. Carla and Lizzie are going to go nuts over you, like everyone else. Petey is only six months old, but I bet you get a few cute giggles out of him, too." They stopped in front of the door, and Jax knocked.

Carla swung it open and smiled at him while holding Petey in her arms. "I'm so glad you came for dinner, Jax." She glanced down at Ace. "Oh, look! Tim told me about him. He's so sweet! Come on in, both of you. Lizzie is playing in the living room. I told her you were bringing a friend, but she hasn't met any puppies before. His name is Ace, right?"

"Yup," Jax said as he leaned over and kissed her on the cheek. "You're looking as beautiful as ever, Carla, and Petey gets bigger every time I see him."

"You're such a sweet talker, Jax," she laughed. "Tim is running late, but he should be here any minute."

Ace marched right in, spotted Lizzie sitting on the floor, and rushed over to her. He started licking her face and hands and toes with his little tail wagging furiously, and Lizzie giggled with glee.

Jax laughed. "Okay, that's enough, Ace. Let poor Lizzie breathe." He lifted Lizzie up into the air and gave her a hug.

But she leaned over in his arms and pointed to Ace. "Doggy."

"Swell, he's going to get all the attention now." Jax set her down and plopped himself in the chair.

"Stop pouting," Carla told him. "She's only two years old. Here, why don't you hold Petey while I check on dinner? You're still the apple of his eye. Did you want something to drink?"

"No, I'm fine." He took Petey from her and set him on his knee to watch Lizzie play with Ace. "That's a great Christmas tree. When did you get it?"

"Last week, don't you remember? Tim had asked you to come with us so you could get one, too."

"I don't have time for stuff like that."

Carla eyed him for a moment.

"Do I smell spaghetti and meatballs?" he asked, changing the subject.

"Yes, I know it's one of your favorites." She went into the kitchen, which had a pass-through opening in the wall so she could still see him. "Tim told me what happened at the bank on Wednesday, Jax. It broke my heart just hearing about it. Are you going to be all right? I know you loved your job, and you and Tim made such a great team. He's not happy about it at all, but he understands."

"I'll be fine, Carla. Do you need any help in there? I signed up for a cooking class and had my second lesson today. So far, I made some pretty decent crepes and hollandaise sauce."

"You're taking a cooking class?"

"Yeah, our teacher is some French chef."

"What's his name?" she asked.

"It's actually a woman. Chef Dupuis." He heard Carla gasp, and he looked up as she rushed back into the room and stared at him with her dark eyes aghast.

"Mademoiselle Dupuis? Jax, she's the most famous French chef in the world! She has a new cookbook out. It costs a fortune, but I was dying to put it on my Christmas list. I had no idea she was in the city. How on earth did you manage to get into her classes?"

"Whoa, Carla, slow down. I saw an ad in the newspaper and responded to it. Is she that big of a celebrity?"

Tim walked in the door. "Sorry, I'm late." He kissed Carla, wrapped his arm around her waist, and looked over at Jax with a grin. "Well, look who's here? Glad you could make it." He saw Lizzie and Ace together on the floor. "No greeting hug from my daughter?"

"Nope," Jax said. "Even your son is more interested in Ace than us."

Tim went over and picked Lizzie up, but she started squawking and pointing at Ace. "Okay, okay." He set her back down.

"See? We might as well be invisible."

"Jax was just telling me about his cooking class, Tim," Carla said. "His teacher is that famous French chef I was telling you about. The one who has a new cookbook for sale that I'm dying to get my hands on."

"The cookbook that costs more than I make in a month?" Tim snipped.

"I know it's too expensive, but I can't believe Jax got into one of her classes."

"I can't believe he's taking cooking lessons." Tim suddenly looked over at Jax and started laughing. "Wait a minute, *her* classes. Your teacher is a woman, Jax?"

"Yeah, so?"

"And how many female students are in your class?"

"I don't know, eight I guess." He scowled. "That's not why I'm taking the class!"

"Sure, it isn't, pal."

"That's enough, Tim," Carla scolded. "I'm impressed that Jax wants to learn how to cook. I wish you would show more interest in helping around the house." She flashed Tim a disapproving glance. "Dinner is ready." She took Petey and went into the kitchen.

"You're a sly dog, Jax," Tim chuckled as he gathered Lizzie in his arms and followed behind Carla.

Jax shook his head. "C'mon, Ace. You're going to love Carla's homemade meatballs."

They enjoyed their meal together, with Petey sitting in Carla's lap, Lizzie in a highchair making a mess, and Ace gobbling up his plate on the floor as though he hadn't eaten in months. Jax couldn't compliment Carla enough for the delicious dinner, and when they finished, Tim and Jax washed the dishes while Carla went down the hall with the kids to get them ready for bed.

Jax found Ace curled up beside Lizzie when he and Tim entered the kids' bedroom to say goodnight. Carla thought it was so sweet and told him to leave Ace where he was until they were ready to go home. So, Jax kissed Lizzie goodnight, pecked Petey on the forehead in his crib, and made his way back into the kitchen.

He sat down at the table and pulled the poker chip out of his pocket. He stared at it for a minute, wondering again why someone had tucked it into the nutcracker. Then, he placed it between two fingers on his left hand and slowly tried to maneuver it in and around each of his fingers to his pinky and back again. It wasn't as easy as it looked, and he tried again.

Tim walked into the kitchen, opened the icebox, and grabbed two bottles of Jax's homemade beer. He turned around and watched Jax for a minute. "You know who you remind me of sitting there twiddling with that poker chip?"

"Who?"

"Tony *T-Bone* DeLuca. Remember him? We caught him and his brother red-handed with a pile of cash after they robbed that nightclub near central park."

"Oh, I remember," Jax said as he kept flipping the clay chip between each finger and getting better at it. "Both he and his brother were sentenced to fourteen months in Sing Sing. According to my calendar, they got out a few weeks ago."

Tim handed him a beer and sat down. "What are you getting at?"

"Murph, I know how the crooks got into the department stores, at least two of them. I told you that there was a small hole in the back door window at Bendel's. I found a similar hole in one of the basement windows at Macy's. Both are perfect circles the size of a quarter, which tells me that they used a precision glass cutter. All they needed to do was slip a string or wire through the hole to unlock the door and the window. The holes are small enough to go unnoticed. Tony T-Bone used the same tool to get into the nightclub."

"What about the other store, Abraham & Straus?"

"I couldn't find anything in the windows on the ground floor, and they didn't have a regular door in the rear of the building, only a large garage door for loading and unloading merchandise. Hauling a ladder around to get into the upstairs windows would have been too obvious and cumbersome. I have another idea, but it sounds too crazy to even say out loud."

"You're talking to me, Jax. Give it a shot."

"Okay..." He stuck the poker chip back in his pocket and took a sip of beer. "There's a narrow metal ladder attached to the wall on the west side of the building for easy access to the skylight above the main corridor of the store."

"You're right. That does sound crazy. You're thinking they climbed up there and cut a hole in the skylight? Then what? It's at least three or four stories to the ground."

"The skylight is comprised of small sections of glass. They just needed to remove enough of the glass so someone could slip through, shimmy down a rope to the main floor, and open one of the entrances. Easy as pie if you think about it. No one would be the wiser about the hole in the skylight, not until it rained or snowed, and people on the main floor started getting wet."

Tim contemplated his theory. "And they knocked the two guards out while they loaded up the merchandise and made their getaway."

"Exactly. After Bendel's was robbed, no one suspected there would be another burglary, let alone two more, so no need for additional security at that point."

"I agree this looks like one of DeLuca's capers, except for one thing, Jax. We found out this afternoon that in all three stores, they only stole toys, board games, dolls, bicycles, train sets, Lincoln Logs, tinker toys, and so forth. That doesn't sound like DeLuca's style at all. As far as we know, he's only gone after the biggest cash payouts."

Jax leaned back in his chair. "Stealing toys doesn't sound like a crime any adult would commit, Murph, except for that legendary character Robin Hood who stole from the rich to give to the poor."

"Who?" Tim asked.

"Never mind. I think we should talk to Lieutenant Simmons about it first thing Monday morning. I was tempted to climb up that metal ladder and take a look at the skylight myself, but I worried about getting arrested for trespassing or some other stupid charge. You put that idea in my head when you told me to be careful about snooping around."

"Well, that's a first. You never listen to me. I guess it can't hurt to pass this by the lieutenant and see what he thinks."

8

Payback

Sunday, December 18

Ace started growling when they were still in bed early the next morning.

"You need to go outside now?" Jax asked. "It's pitch dark out, Ace. Well, you're on your own. Just use that rubber flap we installed in the door yesterday." Jax set him on the floor, and he scampered out of the room. "I guess you really had to go."

Within minutes, Ace raced back into the room. Jax picked him up and put him on the bed, but Ace started barking wildly. Jax scolded him a few times and grumbled under his breath a few more times. Finally, he turned the nightstand light on.

"Ace! What the heck are you..."

Ace ignored him and kept barking and growling at the bedroom window.

Jax sat up, watching him. "What is it?" He flicked the light off, threw his covers aside, and went over to look out the window. "I don't see anything."

Ace wouldn't stop barking, so Jax put him on the floor again and followed him into the living room. Ace kept barking at the back door without using the rubber flap. Jax turned the lamp on and opened the door. Instantly, Ace quieted and walked outside to the end of the brick building, which was only two feet away since his apartment was the last one.

Jax went along with him and peeked around the corner.

A man in a trench coat stood beside the row of bushes, smoking a cigarette. It was too dark to see if it was the same man in the black suit who had followed them at the department store, but it didn't matter. The fact that someone was following him proved his theory about the robberies wasn't far off.

Jax backed away out of sight before whispering to Ace, and the two of them went inside. After he closed the door, he grinned at Ace. "I never thought I'd hear myself say this since I'm a pretty logical guy, but after meeting you, I'm starting to believe in fate and destiny and all that crap. It's like the two of us were meant to run into each other." They headed for the kitchen together. "When we went shopping yesterday, I picked up a Good Housekeeping cookbook. I also bought some eggs and a nice steak to split between us, so let's see if I can scramble us up a good breakfast. If we're going to go broke, we might as well go down in style. Later, I'll give Murph a call, and we'll ditch that guy outside."

At seven-thirty, Jax and Ace slipped out the back door. They snuck along the rear wall of the apartment building, crossed the narrow path midway down, and ended up on Cumberland Street, the next road over. From there, they walked to Fulton Street, and Tim was waiting for them just outside of his apartment building.

"Why didn't you tell me last night that someone has been tailing you?" Tim asked.

"I wasn't sure until this morning when Ace woke me up. As soon as it got light outside, I could see it was the same guy as yesterday," Jax told him. "Boy, for a little tyke, Ace is smarter than the both of us combined. So, Lieutenant Simmons called you into work on a Sunday?"

"Yeah, in case we're needed to help with the department store investigations. I could use the extra hours, anyway. I told the lieutenant that we wanted to speak with him, and he said he'd be waiting in his office. You need to tell him what you told me last night, especially now that we know someone is following you."

When they reached the precinct, Jax was glad it was Sunday and only a few of his fellow officers would be around. He hadn't seen or talked to any of them since he left the force on Thursday. He wasn't on the best of terms with a few of the men, but they all loved to gossip, and he wasn't up to chatting with them, answering questions, or discussing what had happened at the bank.

"I hope those two blockheads aren't in the office," Jax said.

"I doubt it. Stan and Butch never volunteer to work more than they have to."

On the second-floor landing, Jax put Ace down, opened the door, and hesitated. The main office was packed with officers. It looked busier than a regular workday. "What's going on?"

Tim was shocked, too. "I don't know. Just head for the lieutenant's office, Jax."

As the three of them walked down the aisle in between the rows of desks, some officers quickly greeted him, but the rest merely lifted their heads and stared.

"Keep walking," Tim whispered to him when they approached Butch and Stan sitting at their desks.

But Butch caught sight of them. "What the hell are you doing here, Diamond? I thought you quit the force." Then he burst out laughing. "Hey, fellas, get a load of his new ankle-biting sidekick! What a scrawny little thing."

Jax clenched his fists but kept his mouth shut and continued walking until he heard Ace growl. He turned around and saw Ace standing in front of Butch in an offensive position, with his little tail straight up.

"C'mon, Ace," he called to him. "That cornball isn't worth it."

Ace barked at his nemesis and went along with Jax.

The three of them entered the office at the end of the hall. Alma said the lieutenant was waiting for them, but she spotted Ace and started making a huge fuss over him, petting and praising him.

When they entered the other office, the lieutenant motioned for them to shut the door. "Good to see you, Jax. Who's your little friend?"

"His name is Ace. Lieutenant, why is the whole department here on a Sunday?"

"We'll get to that in a minute. I'm more interested in what you have to say right now. Tim told me that you have some information about the robberies."

Jax proceeded to explain about his visits to the department stores and his conversations with the security guard and elevator operator. He described the small openings he found in the windows at Bendel's and Macy's. He even shared his theory about the skylights at Abraham & Straus, and he finished with his suspicions that Tony DeLuca could be behind it. All the while, Jax studied the lieutenant's expression for some sort of reaction, good or bad.

Tim chimed in. "Jax and I put Tony DeLuca behind bars last year for breaking into that nightclub using a glass cutter. We can't figure out why anyone would steal children's toys when there's plenty of valuable merchandise at those stores and dozens of jewelers in the city. Jax even said there's a cash vault at Abraham & Straus, and DeLuca would have been more likely to steal that than anything else."

"Every so often, the salesclerks bundle the money and send it upstairs using a pulley through a hollow pillar," Jax added. "Heck, one of the men's suits at Bendel's store costs a hundred and thirty bucks, so targeting the toy sections in all three stores doesn't make any sense. Still, the information we've gathered is worth looking into."

"I agree," Tim insisted when the lieutenant still didn't respond. "As far as we know, the other departments haven't found any other leads."

Jax started getting angry with the lieutenant's silence while Tim grew nervous. "Lieutenant, I realize this is none of my business," Jax stated firmly. "I also know that these robberies are out of your jurisdiction since the crimes happened in other districts. Still, you have to admit it's too coincidental that DeLuca was released from prison only a few weeks ago."

"Settle down," Lieutenant Simmons said. "I'm just trying to digest everything you've been saying." He got up and opened the second drawer in the file cabinet behind him. He shuffled through it and pulled out a folder. "Let's see. Tony DeLuca was released on November twenty-fourth along with his brother, Dominic. And yes, it looks like they've used that technique a few times before, which explains their short stints in prison." The lieutenant read further. "This is interesting. Did you know their father was an active member of the Five Points Gang in Lower Manhattan? He died in an alley off Liberty Street nine years ago from a gunshot wound. They were a pretty violent group, but thankfully those who survived moved to other cities."

"Sir?" Jax said impatiently.

Lieutenant Simmons closed the folder. "Hang on, Jax." He lifted the telephone receiver and pressed the intercom button. "Alma, would you tell

Officers Collins and Moriarty I need to see them in my office?" He turned his attention back to them. "You may be way off base here, but you're right about one thing. None of the precincts involved have come up with any leads, and we have an even bigger problem now."

"Another robbery?" Jax asked.

"Two department stores were robbed last night, and two men are dead, Officer O'Malley from the Sixth Precinct, and a night security guard at Henri Bendel's store. Three other officers were wounded. They're recovering, but now it's a matter of murder on top of it."

Tim glanced at Jax in disbelief. "They robbed Bendel's again?"

The lieutenant nodded. "They cleaned out the toy department, and the owner has had enough. He shut the entire third floor down, and they're getting rid of their winter display with Santa Claus."

"That'll put a huge dent in their holiday profits, not to mention the loss of inventory," Jax said. "The security guard I spoke to there said the store didn't have enough insurance to cover the first robbery. What was the other department store, Lieutenant?"

"Our burglars are very clever. While most of the precincts have been on alert, we've all been watching the more elite stores in our districts. No one paid any attention to the five and dime."

"The Woolworth Department Store?" Tim asked. "Cripes, their merchandise may not be as valuable as the other stores, but they have the tallest building in the world, and this time of year, they devote three-quarters of their store to children's toys and Christmas gifts. Carla and I planned on doing our shopping for the kids there this coming week."

"Well, you're going to have to put that on hold and see what Charles Woolworth decides to do. All the department store owners are panicking. Captain Ryan said they were calling a meeting this morning to decide if they're going to follow in Henri Bendel's footsteps by closing their toy departments temporarily until the culprits are caught. Police Commissioner Mahoney is up in arms and instructed all precincts to work around the clock until we find those responsible. That's why the main office is full."

"What do you want us to do, Lieutenant?" Jax asked.

He placed the folder on the desk and jotted something down on a piece of paper. "The DeLuca brothers live on Pine Street in Lower Manhattan. Here's their address. Why don't the two of you take Officer MacDougal with you and find out where they were on the nights of the robberies? We would need substantial proof to bring them into the station for questioning, but no matter what the brothers tell you, I'm sure you'll get an idea if they're hiding anything or not."

"I don't think Jax should come along with us," Tim said, earning a scowl from him. "My ex-partner failed to tell you that someone was following him at Abraham & Straus Department Store yesterday, and the same man was waiting outside Jax's apartment building this morning."

"Thanks a lot, *pal*," Jax tossed back. "While that may be true, Lieutenant, I think it's even more important for me to tag along with them. If the DeLuca brothers are behind the robberies and one of their goons is trailing me, then my presence will make them uncomfortable, maybe nervous enough to give us a reason to haul them in."

Lieutenant Simmons smiled. "I should tell you to stay out of it, Jax, but we all know you won't listen to me."

Stan and Butch opened the door and entered the room. "You wanted to see us, Lieutenant?" Stan asked.

"Yes, I'm going to give the Eighty-Fourth Precinct a call and have a couple of their officers check out the skylights at the Abraham & Straus department store in Greenwich Village. I want you and Officer Moriarty to meet them there and let me know what they find."

Butch glanced over at Jax. "What are they looking for?"

"An entry point into the store," the lieutenant replied.

"From the skylight?" Butch squawked. "I can guess who came up with that crazy idea."

Jax stood up and glared at him.

"That's enough, Officer Moriarty," the lieutenant scolded. "We need to follow every lead in these robberies. If you have a better idea, let me know."

"Yes, sir," Butch said. "I mean, no sir, I don't."

Jax suddenly noticed that Ace had disappeared out the open door. "Thank you, Lieutenant. We'll keep in touch." He brushed by Stan and Butch and headed out of the room with Tim following along, but Alma had left her desk and the door into the main hall had been left open, too. "Where the heck did Ace go?"

Slowly, they walked back through the department, looking everywhere for him. Jax was just about to ask a few of the officers if they'd seen him, but he stopped short and started laughing.

"Did you find Ace?" Tim asked, coming up behind him.

"Yeah, look."

Ace had pulled some papers off Butch's chair and was lying on the floor, ripping them to shreds.

Tim burst out laughing.

"What the hell!" Butch shouted. "Get that damn thing out of here! You're going to pay for this, Diamond!"

"Let's go, Ace," Jax chuckled.

Ace dropped the piece of paper in his mouth and happily pranced away in between Jax and Tim.

9

T-Bone

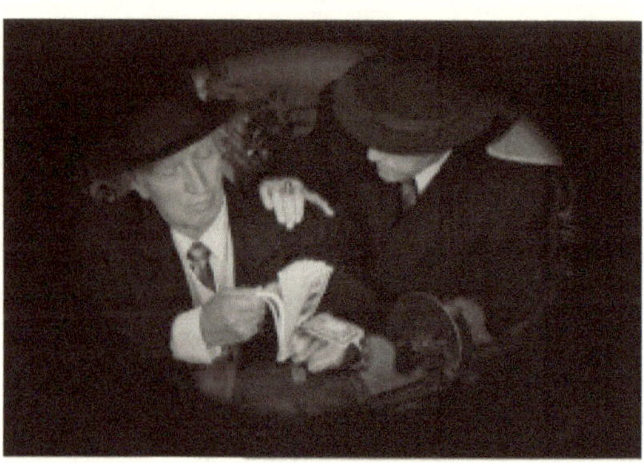

The three of them waited for Jeff MacDougal in the patrol car with Jax and Ace sitting on the passenger side. When Jeff approached, Jax motioned for him to take the back seat.

"Seems weird being back here," Jeff said as he got in.

Tim eyed Jax. "Sorry about that, Jeff, but believe me, there's no arguing with our passenger." He started the car and pulled out onto the road. "Besides, his little partner earned a front-row seat."

"He's a cute little guy. Where are we going, Officer Murphy?"

Jax stared at Tim now. "You make him call you Officer Murphy?"

"He's in training," Tim defended.

Jax rolled his eyes. "We need to talk to a couple of ex-cons in Lower Manhattan, Jeff. And call me Jax. This is Ace."

"Thank you, sir. Who are these ex-cons?"

"Tony and Dominic DeLuca. Officer Murphy and I put them behind bars fifteen months ago, after they robbed a nightclub. We had received a tip from a concerned citizen and caught the two of them with over a hundred grand of stolen money. They were just sitting there counting it when we strolled into the room."

"Whew, that's a lot of dough," Jeff said.

"Yes, it is, and they got off easy as usual."

"The department store robberies are making me really nervous now, Jax," Tim said. "I told Carla we had to wait until I got paid on Friday to go shopping for the kids, but with working extra hours this weekend, we haven't had a chance. If the Woolworth store closes, the nearest one is in Watertown, three hundred miles away. There's no other store in the city that carries affordable toys, and Christmas is only a week away. Rich folks can afford to travel to Philadelphia and Boston to buy their gifts, but what about the rest of us? Jesus, this could shut Christmas down completely for most of the city."

Jeff leaned forward. "No kidding? Woolworths is shutting down?"

"We don't know that yet," Jax told him. "C'mon, Murph, get ahold of yourself. The way to stop that from happening is by finding out who's behind it. So, let's focus on that right now. According to what the lieutenant wrote, the DeLuca brothers live in the same apartment building on the eleventh floor. It's going on nine o'clock, so there's a good chance they'll still be there."

"Let me do the talking, Jax," Tim said. "You're here as an observer to watch their reactions. That's all."

"Yes, Officer Murphy," Jax quipped.

Within ten minutes, Tim parked the patrol car in front of the building and commented that it looked like a pretty ritzy place. Jax told Ace to stay put, and the three of them walked to the main entrance. Once inside, the man behind the front desk lifted his head. So did the man sitting in a chair reading the newspaper on the other side of the lobby, Jax noticed.

"Can I help you?" the desk clerk asked.

"We're here to see Tony DeLuca," Tim replied. "I was told he's on the eleventh floor?"

"Yes, Officer, let me call his suite and see if he's in."

"Don't trouble yourself," Tim replied. "I think we can find it."

Jax let Tim and Jeff walk ahead of him to the elevators while he kept his eye on the man with the newspaper, who had folded it and followed along behind them. Of course, the man motioned to the clerk as he passed by the front desk, and the clerk quickly picked up the telephone. Then, the man got on the elevator with them.

Jax peered over at him. "How are you doing today?"

He merely nodded in reply.

As soon as the elevator doors opened on the eleventh floor, it was easy to tell which room belonged to Tony, since another goon stood in the hallway, guarding the second door.

"We aren't looking for any trouble, gentlemen," Tim announced. "We just want to ask Mister DeLuca a few questions."

The door suddenly opened, and Tony stuck his head out. "Officer Murphy, you should have called and let me know you were coming. I would have dressed more appropriately." He stepped into the hall wearing a maroon jacquard bathrobe. "What brings you to my humble abode on a Sunday morning?"

Tim approached him. "We need to talk to you for a few minutes."

"Of course, come in," Tony said jovially. "As expected, Officer Diamond is with you. Why aren't you in uniform, Jax? Didn't your boss give you enough time to change your clothes either?"

"You're still a jokester, Tony," Jax chuckled as they went into the living room, which was richly decorated with expensive provincial furniture, elaborate holiday decorations, and a Christmas tree filled with colorful ornaments. Jax hung back, standing where he could watch both Tony and his two henchmen standing by the door.

Tony sat down in one of the wingback chairs and took a sip of what Jax pegged as spiked eggnog. "So, how can I help you?"

"We need to know your whereabouts on Wednesday and Friday nights," Tim replied.

"That's easy," Tony said. "My daughter and her husband are visiting for the holidays, and I was right here spending time with them. They'll vouch for me if necessary."

"And last night?" Tim asked.

"Same answer. I assume this is regarding those department store robberies. I can assure you, Officer Murphy. I have far better things to do with my time than stealing children's toys. Besides, I'm fifty-six years old and after my last incarceration, I decided to retire from my previous business."

Tim glanced over at Jax, and he returned with a quick nod, encouraging Tim to continue. "Well, here's the thing, Mister DeLuca," Tim stated. "The burglars relied on a precision glass cutter to enter the premises without detection. That's exactly how you broke into the nightclub last year, and you're the only person we know of who uses that specific tool and technique."

Ah, there it was, Jax thought. That smug and superior expression on Tony's face just washed away.

Yet in its place, the older man appeared almost distressed. His entire body had stiffened, and his hand trembled as he placed his drink back down on the end table. Jax scowled as he quickly glanced around the room again, taking in every detail, the decorations, the Christmas tree, and the family photographs displayed so proudly.

He broke his vow of silence, pulled the poker chip out of his pocket, and went over to sit on the sofa in front of Tony. He leaned forward and placed his elbows on his knees. Then, he blatantly and skillfully maneuvered the chip between each of his fingers on his left hand.

"You have grandkids, don't you, Tony?" he asked, as he continued his performance with the clay chip.

"Six of them."

"Cute kids. I remember watching you do this trick when we questioned you last year."

Tony watched him intently. "Where'd you get that poker chip?"

"Oh, I found it on the street. You know, I didn't realize how difficult your trick was. I can't tell you how many times I dropped it. I've been practicing, though, and I think I've got the technique down pat now. What do you think?"

It took Tony a minute, but he finally grasped Jax's meaning and bolted to his feet. With his abrupt movement, both henchmen stepped forward, making Tim and Jeff pretty nervous, but Tony motioned for his men to back off. "Someone is setting me up!"

Jax stuck the coin back in his pocket. "You're no saint, Tony, and frankly, I'd like nothing better than to put you behind bars again. You're also a family man, and I don't think any grandfather would steal kids' toys at Christmastime. What about your brother, Dominic?"

"I'd shoot him if he tried," Tony growled.

"Okay, I think we're done here, Murph." Jax stood up. "If you have any idea about who could be behind the robberies, Tony, give the precinct a call. Merry Christmas." He followed Tim and Jeff out the door.

"Hey, Jax!" Tony called to him.

He stopped and looked back at the older man.

"I wouldn't be flashing that poker chip around if I were you."

Jax frowned as Tony sat back down in his chair and sipped his drink.

Jeff was practically jumping out of his skin with excitement as the three of them waited for the elevator. "Wow, Officer Diamond…I mean, Jax. I thought we were in a real jam for a minute, but you handled it all so calmly and coolly. What tipped you off that the guy was innocent?"

He broke away from his thoughts. "A couple of things, Jeff. Those photographs of his grandkids, and the fact that he'd spent a fortune decorating his apartment for the holidays. The crooks we're looking for don't give a crap about ruining anyone's Christmas, especially little kids. Another clue was Tony's fedora hanging on the coat rack. Both of his men were wearing the same style. It's pretty customary for thugs to emulate their boss. The guy who was tailing me wore a homburg."

"What's the difference between them?" Jeff asked.

"Both have a crease down the middle, but a fedora is pinched on both sides of the crease and has a flat brim. The homburg has a curled brim."

"Golly, right down to the smallest detail. Do you know who set him up?"

"No, Jeff, we're back to square one." Jax let the two of them get on the elevator first. "Sorry about the wild goose chase. I knew Tony would target the cash, not the toys, but that dang glass cutter threw me off."

"I was convinced of Tony's guilt, too," Tim admitted. "At least we eliminated a prime suspect."

"Want to hear something funny, Murph?" Jax asked. "When I pulled that little stunt back there, it never occurred to me that the crooks could be setting Tony up. I was thinking more along the lines of a copycat, someone who knew about Tony's skill with a glass cutter and had perfected it."

"That's hilarious, Jax," Tim replied flatly. "So, we're in even worse shape than before. We don't know if the crooks used the glass cutter to break into the stores or as a decoy."

"Think of it this way," Jax chuckled as they made their way through the lobby back to the patrol car. "If someone is trying to set Tony up, maybe he'll find them first and take care of the problem for us."

"That's not funny either, Jax."

The three of them got into the car, and Ace went crazy, whining and licking Jax as though he'd been gone for a month. "Okay, okay, next time you can come with us," Jax laughed.

"Where do we go from here?" Tim asked.

Jax finally opened the window so Ace could stick his head out. "There's one nagging question we've been asking ourselves, and the answer to it is the key to solving these crimes. Why toys? Like you said before, Murph, toys are the hottest commodity this time of year, but they're not very lucrative and, frankly, it's just downright mean."

Jeff slid forward and rested his arms on the backs of their seats. "Do you think they're planning something bigger?"

"Hey, you're pretty sharp, Jeff. You hit the nail on the head. While every police department scrambles around trying to stop the robberies and find out who the crooks are, I think those guys are plotting a different kind of heist."

Tim shook his head. "I don't know. That sounds pretty far-fetched. Then again, so does going to all the trouble of robbing four major department stores and only stealing toys, especially when expensive jewelry, furs, designer clothing, and at least one vault full of cash was right there for the pickings. What the hell are they after?"

"That's what we need to figure out, Murph. Let's take a ride over to the Woolworth Department Store. Maybe we can find out what the store owners decided to do after their meeting and take a look around to see how the crooks got into the store. After that, we should scout out some possibilities for what they're planning behind the scenes."

"How do we do that?" Jeff asked.

"We need to check with all the Broadway theaters for any big-name holiday performances. Maybe there's a fancy show at one of the art galleries displaying some famous paintings. Even special nightclub events would be worth looking into. Now that we've eliminated the DeLuca brothers, I also think that we should have a little chat with other suspects."

"Let me guess, Jax, you want to question Orin Marino, your arch-enemy," Tim stated.

"Both Marino and Digger Caputo have been untouchable the past few years. They're both perfectly capable and callous enough to pull this off while being greedy enough to plot an even bigger payoff."

Tim sat there, staring at him. "If you've changed your mind about quitting the force, Lieutenant Simmons probably hasn't finished filling out your resignation paperwork yet."

Jax snickered. "I'm having more fun tagging along with the two of you. It's less stressful."

Tim started the car. "Yeah, well, it seems like you're still in the driver's seat."

"Then why don't you tell us what we should do next, Officer Murphy?"

Tim heaved a sigh and pulled away from the curb. "I want to know if Woolworths is shutting down."

"Great plan." After Jax rolled the window up and relaxed in his seat, he pulled the poker chip out of his pocket and stared at it.

10

Ho Ho Ho

They drove down Broadway and saw three patrol cars parked in front of the Woolworth Building. Tim slowed down and pulled along the curb across the street. "A few officers from the Eighteenth Precinct are talking by the main entrance, Jax. It's tough to miss Officer Brady with his nose stuck in the air. I bet he's still sore at us for letting that poor old drunk go free last month. Brady wanted to throw the book at him."

Jax smirked. "I thought he was going to blow his top when we reminded him that drinking alcohol wasn't illegal, and he couldn't prove the old man purchased the liquor."

"Their precinct probably hasn't heard you're off the force yet," Tim said. "Brady will probably ask why you're not in uniform."

"Let's talk to Officer Agostinelli instead. He's over there by his patrol car." Jax glanced at Ace. "Come on. I'm not leaving you behind again."

They crossed the street and approached Officer Agostinelli. To make it sound more official, Tim told him that Lieutenant Simmons had asked them to take a look around. "We want to help nail these guys, Sam, especially after what happened to Officer O'Malley from the Sixth."

"Yeah, a couple of our men got hurt last night, too, so we could use some extra hands. So far, we haven't come up with anything except an empty toy department. I've never seen anything like this before. Their timing really stinks with the holidays."

"Lieutenant Simmons said the store owners were having a meeting this morning. Have you heard whether Woolworths is going to shut down their toy department?" Tim asked. "I've got a couple of kids, and my wife and I haven't even started our Christmas shopping."

"We heard about the meeting, but I don't know what they've decided."

"We're going to walk around the outside of the building, Sam," Jax said. "Can we get inside the store if we need to?"

"Sure, I've got a key. Just let me know. Hey, what a cute puppy." Sam bent down to pet Ace. "Is he yours, Jax?"

Ace wagged his tail and licked his hand.

"Yup, all fifteen pounds of him," he laughed. "Thanks, Sam."

They headed around the side of the building. Tim explained to Jeff what they were looking for, and all three of them inspected each of the ground-floor windows. The loading docks were in the back, and as soon as they reached the door, Jax spotted the quarter-sized opening in the corner of the window.

Then he noticed the door handle. "Let's go inside. I want to see how they opened the door through that hole."

Within a few minutes, they were walking through the inside area of the docks. Jax scowled when he saw the type of handle on the back door, and he stood there glaring at it for a minute. The door handle at Bendel's was lever-style. So, someone could have easily slipped a loop of wire or string into the small opening and carefully wrapped it around the inside lever. Then, with one taut pull, they could lift the lever up and automatically unlock and open the door. The same was true for the basement window at Macy's. It had a smaller lever-style handle, but a similar concept.

Yet, this handle was a round doorknob, making it impossible to open in that manner.

"What's wrong, Jax?" Tim asked.

"They couldn't have gotten into the store this way, not with the type of door handle. A lever would have worked, but not a doorknob. That gets Tony off the hook for sure, and it proves the holes cut into the windows were just decoys." He tipped his hat off his forehead, placed his hands on his hips, and looked around, thinking.

"Which means they probably didn't break into Abraham & Straus through the skylight," Tim stated.

"These have to be inside jobs," Jax said. "That's the only possible explanation."

Tim shook his head. "But that would mean they planted phony employees at all three stores."

"Think about it, Murph. They pulled off four major robberies without a hitch, baffling every police department in New York City. They're stealing merchandise that's focused on the Christmas holidays, which is likely to shut down the city's entire supply of Christmas presents for thousands of kids. Also, they nearly got away with pinning it on Tony DeLuca. We're not dealing with a few cheesy thugs. This is a group of very shrewd men who have spent a lot of time preparing for this, months probably, making sure everything falls into place for them. Guess what? So far, it has."

Tim nodded. "Good point. Woolworths probably has a long list of employees. I wonder if we could get our hands on it and see if something jumps out at us."

"I doubt any of the office staff are working today."

"Sam Agostinelli has more clout here than we do," Tim said. "If we share what we know with him, he may be able to find someone to come into the office and get us that list. The situation is critical enough to follow any lead, and Sam knows it would be a feather in his cap, too, if we found something."

After they spoke with Sam, Tim was right. The officer readily agreed and went outside to the police call box to find out the number of the supervisor in the personnel department. While they waited, Jax and Ace wandered around the main floor, strolling through the aisles of office supplies, home crafts, and kitchen utensils.

Ace suddenly yipped once, just a soft bark to alert Jax that they weren't alone. Jax looked over and noticed a short, bald man standing by the elevators, posting a notice on the wall. As they walked towards him, Jax read the note.

"Excuse me, sir," he said quietly so as not to startle him. "My name is Jax Diamond. I work for the Thirteenth Precinct. You're closing all the toy departments?"

"Mister Woolworth just informed me that several of the stores in the city are doing the same," the man told him. "He is certainly not happy about it, but until these culprits are stopped, he has no choice. The cost of the stolen inventory exceeds the company's profits for the entire month. It would also take at least a week for a replacement order to be delivered, perhaps longer, and there are only a few shopping days left before the holiday."

"What department do you work in?" Jax asked.

"Accounting on the twelfth floor. My name is Fredrick Duncan."

"Well, Mister Duncan, maybe you can help us. One of my fellow officers is trying to contact a supervisor in the personnel department. We have reason to believe an employee helped the burglars gain entrance into the stores. We need to take a look at your employee list."

"Oh, dear," Fredrick replied as he pulled the ring of keys out of his pocket. "Yes, of course. I have the keys to that department."

Jax told him to hang on while he hurried over to the center aisle. He yelled to Tim and waved him and Jeff over. They followed Fredrick into the elevator and rode to the tenth floor, where Fredrick opened the door to the personnel department. He knew exactly where the files were kept and opened the top drawer.

"There are quite a few," Fredrick told them. "The first three drawers are current employees and the last two contain previous employees who have left the company either of their own accord or at our request. I trust the information in these files will remain confidential. Should you need further information, you can reach me on the intercom." He pointed to the desk telephone. "I will leave my number for you."

"Thank you, Mister Duncan," Tim said. "We appreciate your help."

Jax pulled out a stack of folders from the first drawer and sat down at the conference table behind them. Both Tim and Jeff did the same, and they all began scanning through the paperwork.

"Exactly who are we looking for?" Jeff asked.

"Let's pull out all the newer employees," Jax told him. "Anyone hired within the past six months or so."

"Those working behind the scenes, like in the loading docks, would be good candidates since they'd be more likely to work after the store closes," Tim mentioned.

The three of them spent the next two hours trying to narrow the list down. Jax thought Tim's idea had been a good one, but everyone who worked in the stockrooms and loading docks had been working for the company for at least a year. There were only a few exceptions, yet they were all under eighteen years old and still in school. They also eliminated newly hired men and women who were married with children.

"We still have some possibilities left," Jeff said, pointing to the small stack in front of them.

Jax leaned back in his chair, folded his hands in front of him, and heaved a sigh. "We're missing something."

They all fell silent for a moment.

"We eliminated Woolworth's security employees," Tim said. "What about that security guard you talked to at Abraham & Straus, Jax? You said he was hired by an outside company. Their records wouldn't be included with the store's employees."

"Maybe..." Jax muttered. "Although the stores didn't hire extra security until after the first robbery." Tim's statement led him to another thought, and he shot to his feet. "I know what else is missing. Who is the most important part of the toy department at Christmas?"

"Santa Claus!" Jeff blurted out.

Jax chuckled. "That's right, Jeff. Did either of you run across the file for the employee who dresses up as Santa? I didn't."

"Neither did I," Jeff said.

Tim shook his head. "Nope. Boy, that would really stink if they planted crooked Santas in the stores."

"Yeah, I agree, Murph, especially since I could have sworn the Santa Claus at Bendel's was the real McCoy. Let me call our accountant friend upstairs. Maybe he knows the name of the man hired at this store."

Fredrick joined them within a few minutes. "I apologize, gentlemen. I neglected to give you the files for those hired externally." He went over to the third file cabinet and pulled out the folders. "There are six independent contractors."

Jax took the folders and flipped through them. "The extra security guards work for Brinks. They're pretty reputable, but we need to check the other stores to see if they used the same company." He opened the next folder. "Here it is. Joseph Fortuna was interviewed on November twelfth for the Santa Claus position. He signed a contract to work for exactly five weeks, beginning November nineteenth, which would take him right up through Christmas Eve."

Tim was reading over his shoulder. "There's his address. Mister Duncan, would you mind if we paid Mister Fortuna a visit and asked him a few questions?"

"Not if it helps your investigation," Fredrick replied. "I will inform Mister Woolworth about it."

11

In Hot Soup

"You drive like an old man, Murph," Jax complained as they headed to Joseph Fortuna's apartment on Church Street in Lower Manhattan.

"What's your hurry?" Tim asked.

"The situation speaks for itself, doesn't it? You of all people should be in a rush to solve this case so your kids have presents to open on Christmas morning." Then, under his breath, Jax muttered, "I don't want to be late for my class."

Tim rolled his eyes. "You've got to be kidding me. You're worried about getting to your dang cooking class on time?"

"Officer Murphy?" Jeff called to him from the back seat.

"What do you want, Jeff?" Tim snapped.

"I think we're being followed. The car behind us pulled out as soon as we left Woolworths, and they've been tailing us ever since."

Jax turned around. "It's a dark blue Ford. Did you see how many people were in it?"

"Two men. I noticed their car was parked not far behind us. They were just sitting there like they were waiting for someone."

"Good catch, Jeff," Jax told him. "Murph, turn down a couple of side streets, and let's see if they stick with us."

Tim took the first right turn, drove to the next intersection, and turned right again. After a few more turns, the other car went straight ahead.

Jeff relaxed in his seat. "I guess I was wrong."

"Maybe not," Jax told him. "They could've figured out what we were doing. Keep an eye out for them in case they show up again."

"Jax, we've got another problem," Tim said.

"What's that?"

"We're on Church Street now. According to Joseph Fortuna's address, his apartment building should have been on our left, but it was a vacant lot. I'll swing back around in case I missed it." Tim pulled over in front of the empty parcel of grass and dirt between two brick buildings. "Well, this is it."

"If his address is fake, so is his name," Jax stated.

Tim continued driving down the street. "We need to figure out who he is. Let's get the names of the Santas who were hired at the other stores and check them out. If we could just find one of them and take him in for questioning, we might be able to break this case."

"Let's start with Abraham & Straus," Jax said after he glanced at his watch.

Tim eyed him suspiciously. "That's right around the corner from your apartment. You want me to drop you off there, don't you?"

"Do I need to remind you that I'm not getting paid to help you out?"

"Yeah, okay. Call me when you get home later, and I'll let you know if we made any headway. Be careful, Jax. One of those men following us in the car is probably the same guy who's been tailing you."

After Tim dropped them off at their apartment, Jax changed his clothes. Then, he filled Ace's bowl with fresh water and chopped some leftover meatballs that Carla had given to him. He set the plate down, and Ace started gobbling it up. As soon as Jax grabbed his hat and headed for the front door, Ace was hot on his heels.

Jax kneeled down to pet him. "I'm sorry, Ace. I have another cooking class at the hotel, and I can't take you with me. It'll only be for a couple of hours. You've got to be dead tired, anyway. We had a busy day. Finish your lunch and take a nap. I'll be home before you wake up."

Ace barked at him when he started opening the door.

Jax felt bad, but he stuck his index finger in the air. "Stay!" He shut the door behind him. He caught the subway for Greenwich Village and just stared out the window, dumbfounded by these Christmas capers.

The crooks had pulled off a string of the most sophisticated robberies the city had ever seen. Store owners were forced to shut down the most lucrative and essential portions of their holiday business, which would prevent thousands of families from celebrating Christmas in their traditional manner.

Outside of that, with such precision and perfect timing, the crooks had managed to stump the largest network of police departments in the country. Hundreds of skilled law officers were standing around scratching their heads like a bunch of idiots trying to figure out who they were, and how the hell they broke into the buildings. They had blindsided them and disappeared without leaving any sort of trail behind to follow, except for one, and that had proved to be a dead end.

Jax stiffened in his seat. It just occurred to him that only a few officers knew about Tony DeLuca's skill with a glass cutter. He and Tim had discovered the man's special talent last year. After they arrested him, they told the lieutenant and Captain Ryan about it, but that's as far as it went. What put Tony behind bars and made the headlines was the amount of money he'd stolen from the nightclub. The other details were never made public.

These crooks had cut the holes in the glass knowing he would be the one to find them, his own trail of breadcrumbs to keep him busy and out of their hair. The guy following him was simply making sure he gobbled up their bait.

Jax swore under his breath, cursing himself for being duped so easily. His theory about the crooks plotting something bigger seemed even more plausible now, and he hoped Tim would follow up on it.

Jax got off the subway at East Ninth Street. Only a few people were wandering around Greenwich Village since it was Sunday and most of the stores were closed. As he headed down the sidewalk towards the hotel, he suddenly had the prickly feeling of being followed again.

He stopped and turned around. A young couple strolled along behind him, an elderly woman was peering into one of the shop windows, and a handful of others were scattered about. No one appeared suspicious. He glanced across the street and caught sight of Bendel's department store.

The store's Santa Claus entered his mind again. Obviously, he knew Santa was a legend, a children's fable passed down from generation to generation, like leprechauns and the tooth fairy. Yet, the man who Henri Bendel hired to play the part had so perfectly depicted the fictitious character, right down to his real white beard, rosy cheeks, and jolly laughter. It seemed impossible to him that the man was really a vicious criminal, stealing children's presents right out from under them.

As Jax continued walking down the sidewalk, he still had that same chilling feeling that someone was following him. By the time he reached the front door of the hotel, he'd stopped a few more times and even glanced around again before going inside.

He passed by the front desk. "How are you doing today, Harry? We're making Lobster Bisque today. You should join us."

"I wish I could, sir," he laughed.

When Jax entered the room, Ninette stood there, buttoning her white jacket. He nodded his head to her and saw that the rest of his classmates were behind the counter, ready to go. Everyone except for Nancy. He greeted them, took his place, and slipped the loop of his bibbed apron over his head. While he struggled to tie it around his waist, Ninette sauntered over to him and tied it for him.

"Good afternoon, class," Ninette began, standing beside him at Nancy's station. "We will make Lobster Bisque this afternoon. The first step begins with preparing the roux, which is a thickening agent using equal amounts of butter and flour."

"Shouldn't we wait for Nancy?" Jax asked.

Ninette looked up at him. "She called the hotel earlier, Jax, and said she could not attend class today."

"That's odd," he said. "She was so excited about making Lobster Bisque for Christmas. I hope nothing's wrong."

"Let us continue," Ninette stated. "Everyone, place two tablespoons of butter into your pot, turn the heat on low, and let the butter melt." She waited until they all had completed the task. "Now add the same amount of flour and whisk the mixture constantly until creamy. At first, it will smell like raw dough, but as it thickens, the aroma turns into a delightful woody fragrance."

And she continued guiding them through each step, gradually adding seafood stock, milk, sautéed onions and garlic, and chopped lobster meat. When they were finished, they all poured themselves a small bowlful of their own bisque, and everyone was very pleased with the results.

All the while, Ninette remained by Jax's side, demonstrating each step, yet she constantly glanced over at him smiling and, in his mind, openly flirting with him. Finally, she stepped around the counter to face the others. She reminded them that she had a previous engagement tomorrow afternoon, so their next class would be on Tuesday at two o'clock. Mary asked what dish they would be making, but Ninette told them that she wanted it to be a surprise.

Again, Jax tried mingling with the other women while heading for the door, but Ninette stepped in front of him before he could leave. "May I speak with you?"

He threw her a half-smile. "I really need to get home."

"It will only take a moment." When he hesitated, she added quietly. "It pertains to Nancy."

With that, he waved goodbye to the others. "Do you know why she didn't come to class?"

Ninette removed her hat and jacket. "Poor Nancy's father passed away, Jax. I did not want to announce this to everyone, but you were so concerned about her. I spoke to her personally when she called earlier. She sounded quite sad, and I felt bad for her."

"Aw, that stinks. Thanks for telling me. I don't know her very well, but she seems like such a nice person."

"Yes, she does, and she was very sweet to you. I think it would please her very much if you called her and offered your sympathies to her. She would be touched, I'm sure. I will give you her telephone number."

"Sure, thanks," he replied impatiently.

Ninette turned around and flipped through the folder on the desk. "Oh dear, I must have left it upstairs. I have a room on the third floor. Come with me, and I will give it to you."

Jax hesitated. "That's okay. It can wait until our next class. Like I said, I really didn't know her very well."

"Suit yourself," Ninette said. "When my father passed away, I was crushed. The support of others, even those I barely knew, helped me get through that terrible time." She gazed up at him. "You aren't afraid of me, are you, Jax?"

He chuckled uneasily. "No, of course not."

"Then escort me upstairs to my room. I will simply give you her telephone number, and you can leave. I promise. Je promets."

12

Sucker

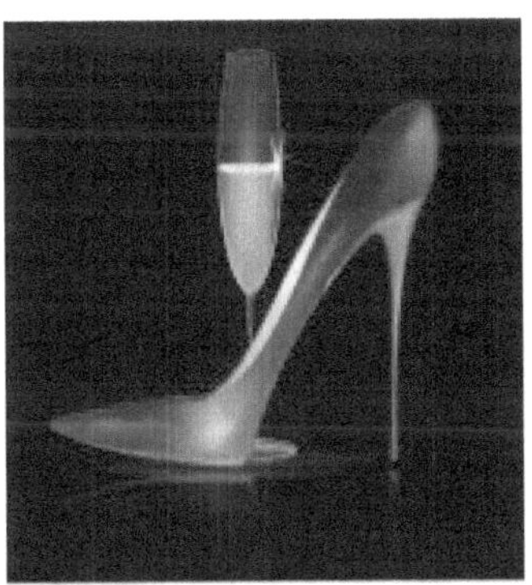

Jax followed Ninette down the hall to the hotel elevators. He didn't know why the woman made him so uncomfortable. It's not like he was inexperienced with women. He's been on plenty of dates. Carla had introduced him to a couple of her friends, and he's met several other women along the way. Maybe he hasn't had a long-term relationship with anyone, but he blamed that on his job and the crazy hours he worked as a cop. That's why he gave Carla a lot of credit for putting up with Tim's hours, especially now that they were raising two kids.

Jax watched Ninette get on the elevator. Outside of being a renowned chef, she was apparently quite worldly and wealthy. She was also stunning, in a dark and mysterious way. So, it didn't make any sense for him to shy away from her.

Yet, she certainly didn't hide the fact that she was attracted to him, and perhaps that was the problem. She seemed pretty pushy, as though trying a little too hard to lure him into the spider's web.

He nearly burst out laughing when an image of that popped into his head.

"While we have a few brief moments together, Jax, why don't you tell me more about yourself," Ninette suggested as they rode the elevator to the third floor.

He shrugged his shoulders. "There's not much to tell."

"Oh, now you are just being obstinate," she scolded. "How long have you lived in New York City?"

"A couple of years. I grew up on a farm north of here. You know, cows, chickens, horses, and acres of cornfields."

She moved closer to him. "How fascinating. It must have been quite an adjustment for you to move to such a large city. What coerced you to leave your hometown?"

"I needed a change of scenery."

"Oh, Jax, darling, another vague answer? At least tell me what you do for a living."

"I'm kind of in between jobs right now," he told her. "That's why it was a good time for me to sign up for your class. I needed something to keep me busy while I look around."

"Indeed? Do you enjoy traveling?"

"I haven't had the opportunity to do much of that." The elevator doors opened, and Jax glanced around. "Your hotel room is the whole third floor?"

"It is the executive suite, Jax. Do not worry. I will keep the elevator doors open for you so you can make a quick escape."

He laughed. "That's okay." He followed her into the living room and walked over to the floor-length windows. "This is terrific. Look at the view you have. That's Washington Square Park, isn't it?"

"Yes. Most people prefer the fancy hotels on Broadway and Fifth Avenue. This is my favorite place to stay when I visit the city. It reminds me of Paris with the quaint shops and intimate cafés." She joined him at the window. "Here is Nancy's telephone number. Would you care for a glass of champagne before you leave? The concierge was kind enough to sneak a bottle to me when I arrived, yet I have not had time to enjoy it."

"Sure, and thanks for her number." He stuffed the paper into his overcoat pocket. While she left his side to open the bottle of champagne, he took off his coat and laid it over a chair. "Can I help you with that?" he asked.

"No, no, I am quite skilled at removing a cork from a bottle of bubbly, as you Americans say." Soon, she stood beside him again and handed him a glass. Then she lifted hers. "Let us make a toast to new friendships, eh?"

He smiled. "Why not?" Their glasses clinked, and Jax took a sip. He wandered over to the mahogany upright piano. He lifted the fallboard, and with his left hand, he played a few notes from Deck the Halls.

Ninette joined him. "You play the piano? See? I told you that you were a man of many wonders. I am anxious to find out what else you are too modest to share with me."

He smirked as he left her side. He took a few more sips of champagne and slowly walked around the room, admiring the holiday knickknacks scattered about. "This is quite a place. It's got to cost at least a hundred bucks a night."

"Who knows?" she replied. "My agent takes care of my travel finances. Speaking of that, I have a job proposition you may be interested in, Jax. After I return home to Paris for a few days, I have a very busy schedule, including trips to Venice, London, and Morocco. You apparently have no ties holding you here, and I could use a man of your...stature, shall we say, to accompany me as my assistant. You will be paid well."

He thought she was kidding and took another gulp of his drink. "Like some gigolo?"

"No, of course not," she scoffed. "I am serious. With your good looks, you could be very beneficial to my business. Do you know how many women worship me? I have sold over a million copies of my new cookbook. What is wrong with having a little fun while we work? I am growing bored with the company I keep."

Jax plopped down in the chair, growing a little woozy from the champagne. "I don't think so, Mademoiselle Dupuis. I'm perfectly happy right here. This city is a great place to live."

"Is it?" she asked. "You have no woman to share your bed at night. You quit your job, and honestly, Jax, you do not appear to be a very happy man."

"Okay, I think this party is over." He set his drink down on the table beside him. "And how do you know I quit my job?" He stood up, but the room started spinning around him. He lost his balance and fell back into the chair. As he struggled to gather his wits, he leaned forward and held his head in his hands. It occurred to him then that the hotel would never give their guests an illegal bottle of liquor. "What the hell was in that drink?"

The woman cackled as she slid the black curly wig off her head and tossed it aside. Then, she ran her fingers through her long, red hair while walking towards him. "Jax Diamond. You're no fool, are you? I played that damn part perfectly, but I was beginning to think you'd never fall for it."

"Who...who are you?" He kept trying to lift himself out of the chair, but it felt like a brick wall had fallen on him, holding him down, and he could barely focus on her.

She moved his drink aside and sat on the end table next to him. "I nearly died of laughter when I saw your name on the list for the gourmet cooking class. Who would've thought that a big, brave city cop like you would want to learn how to cook? You fell right into our laps. Of course, I got a little nervous when you spoke French. I'm glad you didn't press that issue. I only know a few sentences."

"Nancy..." he blurted out, barely able to think, let alone speak.

She reached over and brushed a few strands of blonde hair off his forehead. "Ah, chivalrous, too. I almost wish we had met under different circumstances, Jax. Nancy is fine. You seemed to be getting a little too close to her, so I let her know this morning that our class was canceled. I didn't want you using her as a shield again to avoid me."

With every ounce of strength he had, he snatched her wrist and squeezed it tightly. She yelped in pain, yanked her arm free, and backed away from him.

"If you were smart, you'd be nicer to me. Digger will be here soon, and with the snap of my fingers, he wouldn't hesitate to kill you. Oh, and in case you're wondering, the real Ninette Dupuis always disappears on vacation for a month this time of year. Since no one knows her whereabouts, this was all so simple to pull off. We did our homework."

Jax shut his eyes, fighting against whatever drug she'd put in his champagne. Since he wasn't dead already, he had time to figure a way out of this, if he could just stay awake and get a grip on reality. "It's...not about toys..."

"No, of course not." She went over and poured herself another glass of champagne. "Although before we leave tomorrow afternoon, we'll be setting a few fires around the city where we stashed the toys. That will prevent the cops from following us for a while, giving us plenty of time to leave the country." She lifted her glass to him, took a sip, and laughed. "Stealing the toys was just a game we played to distract from the real treasure, Jax. What a gemstone it is, too. You were the only obstacle in our way. So, Digger cut those tiny little holes in the windows to keep you busy. He knew you would point your finger at Tony DeLuca."

Jax heard the elevator doors open, but he couldn't see who walked in. His entire body felt limp and immobile, although he was more concerned with staying as alert as possible.

"He's right here in the chair, fellas," the woman told them. "Where's Digger?"

"Your boyfriend wants us to take the cop out the back door to the warehouse. He'll meet us there."

The two men walked around in front of Jax. It was a struggle trying to focus on them, but he recognized the man in the homburg hat who had followed him. The other one was her bodyguard from the fashion show, and he stepped forward to tie a cloth gag around his mouth.

"Open the back door for us, Sheila. Come on, Lou, let's get this lug downstairs without anyone seeing us."

Jax had lost all ability to fight against them as they carried him into the other room, through a doorway, and down a couple of flights of stairs. When they went outside, the daylight forced him to close his eyes again, yet the cold air seemed to help refresh his mind a bit. Still, he couldn't move or shout for help.

He expected them to toss him into a vehicle and drive away. Instead, they made sure the coast was clear and carried him in between a few parked cars in the back lot. For a split second, Jax glimpsed something under one of the cars, and he swore it looked like Ace. Quickly, he dismissed that as a hallucination since Ace was back at their apartment. They entered another building, and the two men dropped him on the hard, dirt floor.

"We meet again, Jax."

He peeked up and only saw a blurry silhouette of the man, yet he recognized Digger's voice.

Sheila ran into Digger's arms and started laughing again. "He's pretty hopped up. He drank enough to keep him out of our hair until after we leave the city tomorrow." She looked down at him. "He'll be sleeping like a baby in no time at all."

"Tie him up, boys," Digger told them. "We have a lot of work to do before the luncheon tomorrow. With Jax Diamond out of the way, we're home free."

The two men tied his hands behind his back and wrapped a rope around his ankles. Within a few minutes, Jax heard a door slam, then everything went black.

13

Hope

Monday, December 19

Jax groaned and tried opening his eyes, but his head felt like it was splitting in two. He couldn't move his hands or feet and struggled against the ropes binding him, yet he was too weak and gave up the effort. When he was finally able to see a small portion of his surroundings, everything remained blurry, even his memory of what had happened.

Through the throbbing pain and dense fog in his mind, he heard a faint digging sound, then a grunt. He was lying on his back, and it took tremendous effort, but he managed to move his head to see where the noise came from. He glimpsed something burrowing through the dirt into the room under the wall.

Ace was suddenly on top of him, showering him with wet, slobbery kisses, licking him all over his face. Then Ace grabbed the cloth around Jax's mouth and started tugging at it. He planted his little paws on Jax's chest for leverage and kept pulling at the cloth until it finally slid down off Jax's mouth.

"Good boy, Ace. How the heck did you find me?" He took a few deep breaths. "I need you to untie my hands." Jax winced as he rolled over onto his side. "Not my feet, Ace. My hands, my hands." He wiggled his fingers around to show him.

It took Ace a while, but when he loosened the knot enough, Jax was able to slip his hands out of the noose. He pushed himself into a sitting position and untied the rope around his ankles. Ace climbed into his lap, whimpering, as though sensing what he'd been through. Jax held him close and kissed the top of his head, thanking him.

While he continued petting Ace, his vision began to clear a bit, and he glanced around the room. He was in a huge warehouse with a couple of small windows too high for him to reach and only one set of double doors.

Then he leaned forward, squinting his eyes in disbelief. Nearly half of the warehouse was filled with toys, stretching across the entire back wall with kids' bicycles, red wagons, stacks of different games, and a large assortment of dolls.

"We've got to get out of here."

Ace ran over to the hole he'd dug under the wall.

It hurt to laugh, but Jax started chuckling. "I don't think I'll fit through there."

Slowly and unsteadily, he got to his feet, but he stood there a minute before attempting to take a few steps. He made his way over to the doors and tried opening them, but what sounded like a padlock outside banged against it. Jax pushed and shoved against the doors and even kicked them a couple of times, but he didn't have the strength to break the latch. He turned around and leaned back against the doors, feeling dizzy and nauseous. He worried he was going to pass out again, so he waited a minute, breathing deeply.

When he gathered his composure, he looked around for something he could use to open the door. Then he stared at the wall of toys again. He rushed over and shuffled through them, moving things aside and searching through several boxes. He found a small metal shovel with a wooden handle. In the same box, he pulled out a hammer.

He headed back to the double doors. He turned the shovel sideways to slip it through the crack in between them until it was pressed against the padlock latch. Using the hammer, he pounded the shovel handle, trying to be careful not to break the tools, since they were children's toys and not as sturdy.

Just when the shovel handle split in two, the latch broke free, and one of the doors swung open. He threw the tools down. "C'mon, Ace. We need to call Murph."

As soon as he stepped outside, Jax saw the hotel not far away. Judging from the sun sitting low in the east, he realized it was morning already and freezing out. Yet the chilly air at least helped to snap him out of the doped state he'd been in. He wanted to get as far away from the hotel as possible, so they walked a few blocks until he found a pay phone in front of a little grocery store.

Jax thanked his lucky stars when he discovered he had one nickel left in his pocket. "You not only saved my life, Ace, but you're my good luck charm, aren't you?"

Before he made the call, he glanced inside the store and saw it was ten minutes to eight. Too early to catch Tim at work and too late to catch him at home. He looked at the nickel and dialed the precinct number, praying Tim was there.

But when Tim answered, his good friend started raking him over the coals for not calling him last night and not answering his phone.

"Murph, please," Jax begged him. "I need you to pick me up. I'm on Eighth Street in front of...." He glanced up at the sign above him. "Vito's Groceries. Get here as quick as you can."

Tim sensed the urgency and said he was on his way.

Jax lifted Ace into his arms and nearly collapsed on the bench in front of the store. His memories of yesterday were still a fuzzy mess, although bits and pieces started filtering through. Crucial pieces, like the fact that Digger was behind the robberies, Sheila merely played the part of Ninette, and they were planning some big heist between now and this afternoon.

When Tim pulled up to the curb in the patrol car, Jax carried Ace over and got in. "What the heck happened?" Tim asked. "You look like hell."

"I've been through hell," he said, tipping his head back and closing his eyes. "What a nightmare, Murph. That dame was a phony."

"Which dame?"

"Give me a minute, and I'll tell you everything I can remember. It's important, too, but it hurts too much to think right now. Where's Jeff?"

"I ditched him at the station."

Jax waited a minute. "She slipped some kind of drug into my drink that sent me way over the top. If Ace hadn't found me, I don't know what I would have done."

"Don't worry, Jax. I'll take you back to my apartment," Tim said quietly. "Carla will make you a good breakfast, and we'll get lots of coffee in you."

Jax turned his head to look at him with tears welling in his blue eyes. "Thanks, Murph."

Tim could only nod in return.

After they parked in front of the apartment building, Tim carried Ace and helped Jax out of the car. Carla was just as concerned when she saw the state Jax was in. She set Lizzie and Petey up with some of their toys in the living room, and Ace curled up beside them. She joined Tim and Jax in the kitchen, heated a kettle of water, and made some eggs and toast.

Tim and Jax sat at the kitchen table. While Jax drank a cup of strong coffee, he explained what had happened after the cooking class. The more coffee he got into his system, the more he remembered until he was angrily pacing across the room.

"I should've followed my own instincts. I knew something wasn't right about *Ninette Dupuis*. I even wondered if she had some ulterior motive for insisting that I go to her hotel room, but she was such a big celebrity. What could possibly happen?"

Carla set his breakfast plate down at the table. "That's my fault, isn't it? If I hadn't made such a big deal about her, you wouldn't have fallen into her trap."

He went over and hugged her. "Stop it, Carla. It's not your fault. This woman was a fake and fooled a lot of people."

"It makes me so mad," Carla hissed. "That witch not only impersonated someone I idolize and helped those men try to ruin Christmas for everyone, but she hurt you, Jax. We love you and consider you part of our family."

Jax raised a brow as he glanced over at Tim, but he just shrugged his shoulders. "I love all of you, too, Carla, and I'm fine. Don't get yourself worked up over it."

She finally nodded. "I have a breakfast plate for the hero, too, but he's sound asleep next to the kids."

"Ace deserves a good rest," Jax said. "I can't believe he followed me all afternoon and dug his way into the warehouse. It never occurred to me that he would slip out the back door at the apartment."

As soon as Jax sat down to eat, Ace strutted into the room, wagging his tail.

Carla laughed and set his plate on the floor, then she joined Tim and Jax at the table. "You should get some rest, too, Jax."

"I wish I could, but there isn't time. We have to figure out what they intend to steal that's worth going through all this trouble. Whatever it is, they put a whole lot of planning into it."

"I don't suppose Digger Caputo mentioned giving the toys back to the stores, did he?" Tim asked.

Jax set his fork down. "No." But another piece of his memory just returned. "They're setting fires...a few of them. Sheila said they were going to burn the toys to stop the police from following them. The toys I saw in the warehouse were just a portion of them. I bet those are from Bendel's. That's the closest store. They probably stashed the toys in warehouses near each store. That's how they got away so quickly after burglaries."

"A lot of the warehouses have a single owner who rents them out to different businesses," Tim said. "You said that warehouse was next to the hotel. I'll find out who owns it." He got up and grabbed the telephone receiver.

"Hang on, Murph. Sheila said something else." Jax put his elbows on the table and held his head in his hands, trying to remember. "Stealing the toys was just a game to distract from the real treasure. She called it a gemstone. Then Digger referred to some luncheon today. He said they had a lot of work to do beforehand."

Carla's brown eyes grew wide. "Were your cooking classes at the Hotel Lafayette, Jax?"

"Yeah, why?"

"After you told me that Ninette Dupuis was in the city, I looked in the newspaper to see what engagements she planned to attend. She's hosting a luncheon today at that hotel for a very prominent couple, and about thirty people will be there."

"What prominent couple?" he asked.

"Edward McLean, owner of the Washington Post, and his wife, Evalyn. She's a mining heiress and owns the Hope Diamond. I read all about it. Pierre Cartier sold the diamond to her and her husband for an undisclosed amount of money ten years ago."

"The Hope Diamond..." Tim muttered. "Isn't it supposed to be cursed or something?"

"Yes. It's had several owners who have seen great misfortune," Carla told them. "Edward McLean was hesitant to purchase it, but Pierre Cartier had the diamond reset to better suit Evalyn's tastes, and she never travels anywhere without it."

Jax sat back in his chair. "A gemstone..."

"Yes, and that's not all," Carla said. "Missus McLean never travels without her Great Dane, Mike, either. He's often seen wearing the diamond at a lot of events."

"Whoa, you're kidding me?" Jax laughed. "Did the paper say when the lunch takes place?"

"At noon today," she replied.

"You're wonderful, Carla!" Jax told her. "That's the treasure. Murph, your wife is a genius."

"She certainly is," Tim chuckled. "I'll call the precinct. Between what they did to you and knowing where they stashed the toys, we've got all the evidence we need to put them behind bars."

"Wait a minute, Murph. They doped me up pretty good. I doubt my testimony will stand up in court, not after their lawyers get done with me, and we don't have any proof that they stole the toys. We only know where they put them." He looked at Ace, sleeping on the floor next to him. "I have an idea."

"Oh, crap," Tim grumbled. "I can't wait to hear this."

14

The Sting

"We're going to steal the Hope Diamond before they get their hands on it," Jax said.

"What?" Tim got up and started pacing across the room. "I think that drug they gave you is still twisting your mind up in knots."

"Listen to me, Murph. We know they're going to steal that diamond during the luncheon. We also know Sheila is hosting the lunch, posing as Ninette Dupuis, but Digger wouldn't leave it all up to her, so a couple of his goons will be there, too. After what Carla told us, there's a good chance the Great Dane will be wearing the diamond. The minute we figure out how they intend to steal it, we'll catch them in the act and beat them to the punch. The beauty of it is, they think they're home free. Digger even said that before they locked me in the warehouse."

"It's too risky, Jax. We need to call Captain Ryan so he can handle it."

Jax scowled. "No! I'm not going to let him and his cavalry mess this up. Look at what he did at the bank. I want to nail these crooks to the wall."

Tim stopped pacing and stared at him.

Carla reached over and placed her hand on Jax's shoulder. "Tim, it can't hurt to hear what Jax has in mind. I want to see these people pay for what they did, too."

When Tim didn't say anything, Jax looked over at him. "It's probably a good idea if we have a couple of cops in on this. We'll give Lieutenant Simmons a call. We also need to tell him to check out the warehouses for the rest of the toys, but not yet. I'm not telling him exactly what we have planned either. Have you ever met Digger Caputo?"

Tim shook his head. "Not in person, but he's probably heard my name before."

"That'll work. I have a pal at the front desk of the Lafayette Hotel. I bet Harry would arrange for two extra seats at one of the tables for lunch today. I'll give him a call."

"You can't show up there, Jax," Tim told him. "They'll spot you right away."

"They're for you and Carla. I'm sure you can scrounge up a decent suit, and Carla looks beautiful no matter what she wears. You'll both attend the luncheon as a highfalutin couple."

"Jesus, I'm not letting Carla get in the middle of this!" Tim yelled.

"I can speak for myself, Tim," Carla scolded. "I want to hear the rest of Jax's plan."

At eleven o'clock, Jax was driving the patrol car to Greenwich Village. Carla and Ace were in the passenger seat, with Tim sitting in the back. Jax had a nice telephone conversation with Harry earlier. The man was so accommodating, he decided to fib a little. He told Harry that he was a police officer assigned as undercover security for the McLeans. With that, Harry readily agreed to sneak him into a small storage room off the main dining area where he could monitor the room through the window. After their conversation, Jax pried Tim's police badge out of his hand so he could show it to Harry when he got to the hotel.

Jax glanced in his rear-view mirror. "You could have worn a fancier suit."

"This is the best one I've got!" Tim yelled.

"Okay, okay, don't get all hot under the collar. You look fine, Murph. Or should I say, *Mister Alex Ferguson,* renowned philanthropist?"

"Isn't Alex Ferguson a pitcher for the Yankees?"

Jax snickered. "It was the first name that popped into my head when Harry asked. He needed to put your names on the list. At least I didn't say Chicken Hawks, one of the outfielders."

Tim just shook his head. "I don't even know what a philanthropist is."

"Don't worry, most people don't," Jax assured him. "Besides, you won't be the center of attention. The lieutenant is arranging for two plain-clothes cops from the Sixth Precinct to watch the front and back doors. I told him that we'd call him if our lead panned out. Harry is going to get me into that storage room, so make sure you watch for my signal, Murph."

"Carla and I know what to do, but what about Ace?" Tim asked.

"Don't underestimate him. With only two pups in the room, I'm sure they'll find each other pretty quickly. I just hope that Great Dane is with the McLeans and wearing the diamond. If not, we'll need to figure out pretty quickly how Digger plans to get the gemstone away from Evalyn McLean. We don't want anyone getting hurt." He glanced over at Carla and smirked. "I know you want to scratch Sheila's eyes out, Carla. I do, too. Let's wait until this is over, okay?"

"I'll try to restrain myself, Jax," she told him, but he saw the blood-thirsty look in her eyes and wasn't so sure.

He drove down East Ninth Street and pulled the car into the back parking lot of one of the tenant buildings a block away from the hotel. He wished Carla and Tim good luck, patted Ace on the head, and watched them walk to the main road. Then he stayed close behind the buildings, heading in the same direction.

When he saw the hotel, the first thing that popped into his mind was what had happened yesterday, and how easily he fell into Sheila's trap. He shook those thoughts away since they served no purpose now, and instead, he concentrated on the task at hand. At exactly eleven-twenty, Harry opened the side door and looked around for him. Jax hurried over, went inside, and Harry closed the door.

Immediately, he showed Harry the police badge. "We really appreciate your help, Harry. Mister and Missus McLean prefer added security when they attend events like this. I'm just going to stay out of the way and make sure everything goes smoothly."

"Honestly, I feel better with you here," Harry told him. "I thought it was rather frivolous of the McLeans not to have their own security guards. The storage room is right across the hall. If you need anything at all, I'll be at the front desk."

Jax thanked him and entered the small room. He glanced at the shelves on either side of him, which were filled with folded linens, towels, and other hotel amenities. He approached the other door on the opposite wall and peered into the dining room through the window.

Every table was set pristinely with several pieces of silverware, water glasses, and triangular-shaped cloth napkins standing upright on each plate. Elegant Christmas candles, wreaths, and strands of garland adorned the entire room, and several people were already mingling by the doorway.

Jax made sure the door was unlocked in case he needed to enter the dining room, and he waited there, watching through the window. Within ten minutes, he saw Tim and Carla enter the room, and Tim was carrying Ace. He had to admit they were a striking couple, and they seemed to play the part perfectly, greeting some of the other guests and introducing themselves.

At ten minutes to twelve, he saw the maître de enter the room and heard him ask everyone to take their seats. Tim glanced over at Jax as they approached their table. Tim pulled the chair out for Carla and placed Ace in her lap. Once everyone was seated, another couple appeared in the main doorway with one of the biggest dogs Jax had ever seen.

As the three of them walked to their table not far from Tim's, Jax saw the large blueish gemstone dangling from a gold chain around the beast's neck. Ace had noticed the giant spotted mutt, too. His ears perked up, and Jax began to worry that Ace wouldn't get anywhere near the other dog.

Everyone's attention was suddenly drawn to the other side of the room when a woman entered through the kitchen door. Jax stiffened and glared at Sheila, who wore her chef's costume, white jacket and hat, and a black curly wig. In that fake French accent, she greeted the guests and told them how delighted she was to be their host.

Then, she announced the meal she was preparing for them, beginning with fig and goat cheese tarts, followed by French onion soup, sweet duck breasts with cherry sauce, French bistro salad with Roquefort dressing, and finally a dessert of chocolate mousse.

While she spoke, Carla peeked over at Jax with daggers in her eyes.

Sheila finished her speech and strolled between the tables, heading for the McLeans' table. She talked with the famous couple and said something clever that made them laugh. Yet, before she went back to the kitchen, she quickly flashed her broad smile at the guests sitting in the corner on Jax's left. He pressed his cheek against the window to get a better view.

Right off, he recognized Digger Caputo and Lou, the man in the homburg hat.

His heart started racing, and Tim looked over at him in panic, alerting him that he saw them, too. After Sheila disappeared into the kitchen, Jax kept his sights on the two men.

While they waited for the servers to pass around the first course, several guests got out of their seats to mingle with those at different tables. Jax noticed Digger reach into his pocket, but Jax grew aggravated since didn't have the man in full view. He opened the door slightly, peered through the crack, and watched Digger slip something to Lou under the table.

Lou kept his hands hidden and carefully gathered the gold chain into the palm of his right hand. That's when Jax saw the sparkling blue bauble attached to it and realized they intended to switch the real necklace for a fake one.

He caught Tim's attention and kept nodding his head. Tim quickly told Carla to set Ace on the floor. Jax crossed his fingers, but Ace just stood there. Jax saw Lou stand up and panicked now. Yet, as they rehearsed, Carla quickly told Ace to go see the other dog, and off he went, straight toward Mike, the Great Dane.

Jax, Tim, and Carla watched them intently.

Mike spotted Ace and slowly lowered his head. Then, the two stood there, nose-to-nose for a minute. Lou walked towards the McLeans' table, but Ace suddenly spun around and pranced over to Carla and Tim. Mike followed right along behind him.

Lou stopped when he saw the two dogs together beside Carla and glanced back at Digger, not knowing what to do next.

Jax didn't want to make a scene in the dining room. Now that he knew what they were up to, he hoped Digger and Lou would give up their efforts and head for the exit. Then, he could catch them in the hallway with the fake necklace.

But Ace saw Lou standing there. Instantly, he shifted into his offensive pose with his tail straight up, and he crept toward the man, growling.

"Oh, what the hell." Jax burst through the door and ran towards Lou, tackling him to the floor. "He's got a phony necklace, Murph!"

Everyone got to their feet, shocked at what was going on, and both dogs started barking wildly.

While Jax fought with Lou, Tim ran after Digger, who disappeared out the door.

Jax punched Lou in the gut and face, and the man caught him in the jaw, but Jax finally struck him again and knocked him out cold.

Jax picked up the fake necklace off the floor, got to his feet, and stood over Lou. "Here, Carla, give this to the McLeans and tell them what's going on." Yet, she ignored him and stormed towards the kitchen. "Carla, get back here!"

Frantically, Jax looked around. He told the large man at a nearby table that he was a cop, and he asked him to make sure the thief didn't go anywhere. Then Jax hurried over and dropped the fake necklace onto the McLeans' table, along with Tim's police badge, and he raced into the kitchen after Carla.

But by the time he got there, Carla had already stripped Sheila of her wig and held her snugly in a headlock. Sheila had a cut on her cheek and remained as quiet as a mouse, looking terrified.

Jax chuckled. He grabbed some cooking twine and tied the woman's hands together. "Good work, Carla. Keep an eye on her. I want to make sure Tim's okay."

He hurried down the hall, then slowed his pace when he saw that Tim and Harry had hogtied Digger to a chair by the front desk with a handkerchief tied around his mouth.

"Nice job, Harry!" Jax laughed. "Thanks for your help. Murph, your wife took care of Sheila for us in the kitchen. I'd watch her left hook if I were you."

Within the hour, Jax and Tim stood with Lieutenant Simmons by the front door of the hotel, watching the officers haul the three criminals off to jail. The lieutenant said they found out who owned the warehouses and were bringing him in for questioning. They were also searching each of the warehouses for the toys.

"Are you sure you don't want to change your mind about staying on the police force, Jax?" the lieutenant asked.

He looked at Captain Ryan standing outside, talking with Harry and the hotel manager. "Naw, I'm good, Lieutenant, but thanks anyway. C'mon, Murph, let's go check on Carla and Ace."

All the guests had left, but they found Carla sitting at the table with the McLeans in the dining room. Both Ace and Mike were sleeping on the floor next to one another.

Edward McLean stood up and shook their hands. "I can't thank you enough for stopping those men."

"We didn't want to make a big scene, but my sleeping partner over there had other ideas," Jax said. "I should get him home."

Evalyn smiled. "Mike has taken quite a shine to Ace. Next time we're in the city, we'll have to plan a day when we can get together."

15

Partners

Friday, December 23

"Why the heck does the lieutenant want to see me, Murph?" Jax asked again after Tim picked him and Ace up in the patrol car. "I already told him that I don't want to stay on the force."

"Quit your griping," Tim laughed. "That's not why he wants to see you."

"Then tell me what this is all about! You're supposed to be my friend. Don't leave me in the dark."

"You'll find out when we get to the precinct."

"Cripes, I don't want to walk through the main office again. It didn't go well the last time, remember?"

"Would you relax? What happened to your Christmas spirit?"

"I'm dead broke, and I have no job. You tell me."

"Well, that was your choice," Tim reminded him. "Just think about what we accomplished. We caught the bad guys before they got their hands on the Hope Diamond, and we put them behind bars for a long time. The department stores recovered their merchandise and opened the toy departments by Wednesday morning. The three of us, excuse me, four counting Carla, literally saved the

Christmas holidays for the entire city. You should feel really good about it. I know I do."

"After all that, the lieutenant shouldn't be dragging Ace and me out of bed so early in the morning."

Tim laughed and refused to say another word.

After Tim parked the car, Jax carried Ace up the stairs to the second floor of the precinct. As soon as he opened the door to the main office, all the officers were on their feet, clapping and cheering him.

Jax was stunned. "What the heck is going on?"

"Think of it as a little going away party," Tim chuckled, pushing Jax into the room.

Jax scowled as he carried Ace and reluctantly walked down the aisle, but everyone kept congratulating him and patting him on the back as they went by. Even Butch and Stan were on their feet, clapping. Finally, Tim opened the door to the reception area and led him straight through to the adjoining office, where both Alma and the lieutenant were waiting for him.

"This was unnecessary, sir," Jax told him.

The lieutenant smiled. "We know you hate fanfare, Jax, so I'll keep it short and sweet. Here is your reward for solving this case." He handed Jax a check. "The department stores showed their gratitude for retrieving the merchandise by making a sizeable donation to the New York City Police Department. Mister and Missus McLean insisted upon rewarding you, Ace, and Officer Murphy personally for stopping Digger Caputo and his gang from stealing the Hope Diamond."

Jax stared at the check for one thousand dollars in disbelief. "You're kidding me?"

"Lieutenant Simmons gave me a check yesterday," Tim said. "I had a heck of a time trying to keep it a secret from you. It's a great going away gift, huh?"

Jax was speechless.

The lieutenant kept his eyes on Jax. "I'll say it one more time. I wish you'd stay on the force, Jax."

He looked up at him and smiled. "Actually, Ace and I were thinking about starting our own private detective agency. You put that idea into my head when I quit my job. Ace sure as heck proved he's a great partner. This money will really help to get it going. So, I'm sure one way or another, we'll be working together again soon."

The lieutenant laughed. "I look forward to it, Jax."

"Yeah, I'm sure Captain Ryan will be thrilled about it, too," he chuckled.

Half an hour later, Jax was still staring at the check while he and Tim walked out of the station. "You know what, Murph? Maybe there is a Santa Claus."

"Hey, speaking of that, I meant to tell you. They found three fake Santas who helped Caputo and the others get into the department stores. The man Henri Bendel hired to play the role of Santa wasn't part of their gang. Apparently, they've hired the same man for years. He lives alone in a small apartment near Coney Island and is a real sweet guy."

"So how did they break into that store?" Jax asked.

"Digger's right-hand man, Lou, started dating one of the salesclerks there. She let them inside. C'mon, I'll take you and Ace back to your apartment."

Jax looked at Ace in arms. "Can you take us to Greenwich Village instead, Murph? We're going to do a little shopping."

Tim dropped them off in front of a row of shops in the village. He said he'd see them tomorrow for their Christmas Eve dinner together and drove away. Jax and Ace walked down the street, but Jax stopped in front of Bendel's department store.

"I want to show you something, Ace," Jax told him.

They entered the front door, and the store was mobbed. Jax carried Ace upstairs to the third floor. He heard the children's choir and headed to the back of the department. He smiled when he saw the line of children waiting to see Santa. He moved closer, set Ace on the floor, and leaned against the wall, just watching them for a while. One by one, the children had their turn on Santa's lap and walked away smiling, knowing their Christmas wishes would come true.

But Santa suddenly stopped the next child from coming forward. He looked over at Jax and motioned to him. Jax turned around, thinking he was waving to someone behind him, yet no one was there. When he turned back around, he saw Ace prancing away toward the jolly, bearded man. Santa whispered to one of his elves, then he took the small stuffed reindeer from him and gave it to Ace, who wagged his tail excitedly.

Again, Santa wiggled his finger at Jax until he curiously and uncomfortably walked over with all the kids and parents staring at them. Santa grabbed one of the wooden nutcrackers off the shelf and handed it to Jax. Then, Santa winked at him and called to the next boy waiting in line.

Jax wandered away, dazed by what had just transpired, while Ace happily carried the stuffed animal in his mouth.

When they finally made their way out the front doors, Jax looked up. It was snowing outside for the first time this year. Just a gentle fluttering of white flakes floating around them. "Like I said all along, Ace. That Santa is the real deal."

By the time they reached the subway, Jax had a new destination in mind, and they boarded the train for Linden Cemetery on Second Avenue in Manhattan. With no idea where the plot was, Jax strolled around the cemetery, confident that they would find it.

Then he saw a large Christmas wreath entwined with a yellow ribbon with Jonah Rivera's name printed on it, the boy who died at the bank.

Jax kneeled beside the grave and inhaled a few deep breaths before speaking. "When I was a little older than you, a woman stopped me on the street and gave me a nutcracker like this one." He looked at the statue in his hands. "She told me that I was being a very brave soldier, and she disappeared from sight." Jax stood the nutcracker beside the wreath. "You were a very brave soldier, Jonah. I'm sorry."

Jax finally got up and wiped the tears from his eyes. As he walked away, he noticed Ace wasn't with him. When he looked back, he watched Ace place his stuffed reindeer on the ground beside the nutcracker.

Jax smiled. "C'mon, Ace. Let's go buy Lizzie and Petey lots and lots of toys." The two of them headed out of the cemetery, and Jax started laughing. "Hey, here's a great idea. Why don't we buy Carla that new cookbook by the real Ninette Dupuis? She'll be madder than hell at us when she opens that gift! But what should we get for Murph?"

Ace barked.

"Great idea! Let's buy him a snazzy new suit. He looked like a bum at that luncheon. We should probably pick up a cheap car, too, somewhere. If we're going to be detectives now, we need to look like professionals. Boy, we're going to have fun, Ace. Merry Christmas, partner."

The ~~End~~ Beginning

A Special Note to Readers

gailmeath.com[1]

Thank you very much for reading *Two of a Kind*. I hope you enjoyed it. If you've read the other books in the series, you'll see that I'm trying to use a different theme in each book. *Songbird* focused on Broadway Theaters. *Framed* was all about bootlegging and gangsters. *Deuce* took us to Laura's small hometown in Millbury, and *Two of a Kind* deals with a few of the larger department stores in New York City at Christmastime. The next book, *Blackjack*, well, that speaks for itself, and we're back on Broadway with a full cast, including my favorite gangster/friend, Orin Marino.

I always enjoy sharing historical tidbits and songs from the era. This book doesn't include any songs, but since it's about Christmas, I thought I would share a few holiday tunes. The first video isn't really a song, but it made me laugh, and it was released in 1922. The second video took me back to my childhood at Christmastime. The music was a staple in our house during the holidays, and I couldn't pass up sharing Bing Crosby's infamous *White Christmas*.

Santa Claus Hides in the Phonograph by Ernest Hare, 1922
https://www.youtube.com/watch?v=QNb16W-bnMI&t=76s
The Nutcracker Suite – by Tchaikovsky, 1892
https://www.youtube.com/watch?v=M8J8urC_8Jw
White Christmas – Bing Crosby, first recorded in 1942
https://www.youtube.com/watch?v=EwKc05_6ItY

---

1. https://www.gailmeath.com

While looking up cookbooks in 1921, I ran across *Everywoman's CookBook* which was published in 1922. Love the title and the cover! It was first published by the National League for Woman's Service and "includes menus, suggestions for pairings, and over ninety recipes that reflect a turning point in home cooking." Helen Wells, the author, also adapted recipes for prohibition.

I am not a gourmet cook, but for fun, I decided to post a few of my favorite recipes on my website, some passed down to me from my Polish grandmothers. Just a small variety of recipes if you'd like to take a look at them.

Writing any historical novel takes a great deal of research, right down to using the proper words and phrases of the times with special care not to use more modern terms that weren't in existence yet. In this book, I mentioned *get-out-of-jail-free cards*, so I needed to find out if the Monopoly game existed back then.

Surprisingly, the history of *Monopoly* can be traced back to 1903, when Lizzie Magie, an American antimonopolist, created a game that she hoped would explain the single-tax theory of Henry George. It was intended as an educational tool to illustrate the negative aspects of private monopolies. She took out a patent in 1904. Her game, *The Landlord's Game*, was self-published in 1906, and it was played similarly to the version we're familiar with. Here is what the original board looked like:

Briefly, a few more interesting facts. The Woolworth Building in New York City was the world's tallest building from 1913, the year it was built, to 1930, and it cost thirteen and a half million to build. As a nickel-and-dime store, that surprised me when you place it alongside money giants like Macy's and Abraham & Straus (they were co-owned), Saks, Bloomingdales, Gimbels, Lord & Taylors, and Bonwit Teller. When Frank Woolworth died in 1919, there were 1,057 Woolworth stores in the United States and Canada, plus another 175 stores in England.

Lastly, the facts about the Hope Diamond in the book were true. The diamond was owned by Edward (Ned) and Evalyn McLean. They were hesitant to purchase the notoriously cursed 45-carat blue Hope Diamond in 1911, but Evalyn was determined to own it. So, Pierre Cartier reset the diamond for her, and Evalyn often let her Great Dane, Mike, wear the gem on his collar at public events.

Evalyn never believed in the curse and owned the diamond for the rest of her life, but she suffered some bad luck over the years. Her husband ran off with another woman, her son was killed in a car accident, and her daughter died of a drug overdose.

One article I read stated that Princess Diana had owned the diamond for a time, but I couldn't find anything to confirm that. The diamond is now in the

Smithsonian Institution, and it's worth is estimated at three hundred million dollars.

Thank you again for your time and support! If you enjoyed *Two of a Kind*, I hope you will take a moment to leave a review on your favorite retailer. I would greatly appreciate it.

All my best, Gail